Veneri Verbum

Book 1 of the Figments series

ZANZIBAR 7. SCHWARZNEGGER

Text copyright © 2015 Zanzibar 7. Schwarznegger

Cover photo and artwork copyright © 2016 Chizzy Press

Printed in the United States of America.

First printing, 2015.

ISBN 9780692370346

10 9 8 7 6 5 4 3 2

For Izzy

Special thanks to all the plot bunnies and the NaNoWriMo group on Facebook.

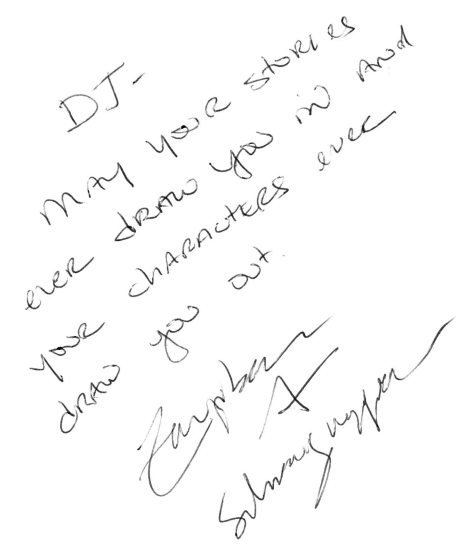

Table of Contents

HASHTAGS

Christopher Cullum had a problem. He was pretty sure normal people didn't fall in love with characters they made up.[1] Strike one for being normal.

Christopher was lying on his back in his unmade bed on a cool November night, sketching bad drawings of his favorite (and only) character. He was on his seventh sketch of the night. He spread the sketches out and looked them over. The first was Elsa happily working in a garden. The second was just half of Elsa's face; the rest was hidden inside a hood as she shyly avoided looking toward him. He didn't like the third one: she was sitting with her arms folded across her chest and a scowl on her face. He couldn't picture her scowling. Not his Elsa.

The fourth picture had her curled up in bed, eyes half-closed, on the verge of falling asleep. The fifth was his favorite: she was balancing on top of a fence post, arms outstretched, a goofy expression on her face. The sixth caught her midsneeze, nose red from a cold. Now he was drawing her curled up with a book. She was far smarter than he was and read often, although he'd had to ask some online friends for ideas of what she would be reading.[2]

He'd been drawing for almost four hours instead of writing. He had a haphazard tower of empty energy drink containers, a couple of empty potato chip bags, and a queasy feeling in the pit of his stomach to show for it.

He sighed, sniffing at the paper. The second strike against normality might be the way that he could sometimes not just see Elsa (it was a popular name at the time), but could also hear her voice, just a little bit husky and throaty, and smell her, a weird blend of vanilla latte and cinnamon that reminded him he should really stop writing in coffee houses. Since it was a nice escape

---

[1] Normal people fall in love with characters other people make up.

[2] Group brainstorming is credited with innovations like Wikipedia, but is also the official cause for the group flatulence experiment at the community college in Wooley, Montana, that resulted in the obliteration of an entire town no one ever knew existed.

from living with his parents and being asked on a regular basis when he was going to stop messing around with writing, get a real job, and move out, he continued to write characters who smelled like coffee.[3]

Christopher was exactly in his mid-twenties. He was neither particularly good-looking nor particularly bad-looking. He had sandy brown hair, a bit mussed, worn however it happened to fall over unremarkable brown eyes. He was exactly the current average height for an adult male and just a bit on the skinny side. He worked flipping burgers part-time, attended college when he remembered to sign up for classes, and scribbled unfinished stories in the margins of his homework.

This year was going to be different. It was his first time participating in NaNoWriMo[4] and he was going to finish an entire novel, get published, and change his life. He traced the outline of his drawing of Elsa. As soon as he finished this one, he would go back to writing his introduction. So far, he had a lot of background about Elsa, but not much else. Not that it mattered to him. He was madly in love with Elsa's multiple braids that sprouted beads in random places and her toenails each painted a different color. *She* mattered to him.

He pushed away the small part of his head that reminded him she wasn't real. He wasn't letting that stop him. He didn't have a real girlfriend anyway, so it didn't hurt to send love notes to Elsa every time he sat down to write. He set aside the drawing of Elsa and pulled up a spreadsheet on his computer, adding "small birthmark on left shoulder" to his database of physical details.

He sat at the keyboard, waiting for the words to flow. When nothing happened, he wrote a quick love poem to Elsa in his notebook:

---

[3] Vladamir Koripsky wrote during his lunch break while working at a waste treatment facility. His characters had an unfortunate tendency to smell like raw sewage.

[4] NaNoWriMo is often abbreviated to NaNo, not to be confused with NoNo (unless you live in India).

I like your hair.

I like your toes.

But most of all

I like your nose.

He had a notebook full of poems and notes like that, but only three hundred forty-seven words of story. According to plan, he should have around five thousand words, but he was a bit behind. Maybe he should make the notes into a story.

He turned back to his drawing, caressing the page as he erased an errant line. The nose was too long and the mouth was too small and she resembled more of a fat potato than a vegan goddess, but he could see her in the picture anyway. If he squinted, the nose shortened into a cute little pug (*too short*, she complained inside his head, so he left it to add a flaw to her character) sprinkled with freckles she also hated. Her mouth widened, framed by laugh lines because he thought she was the funniest thing since Felicia Day. No red hair, though. Red hair was pretty cliché. Instead, she had black hair and brown eyes and multiple tan lines on her feet because she never wore the same sandals two days in a row.

He sighed and stroked her penciled cheek. His head spun and he wished he hadn't had that last energy drink. He closed his eyes to stop the spinning, keeping them closed until he heard someone clearing his throat. Or her throat. It didn't matter, really, who it was. Someone was in his room.

He opened his eyes.

There *was* someone in his room, sitting backwards on his desk chair, legs over the seat back with her feet dangling lazily, staring at him.

He rubbed his eyes. No. *Elsa* was in his room, sitting on his desk chair, staring at him. He blinked. "I thought I could hold off insanity at least until I hit my fifties. Then I'd be an eccentric writer. I don't think it works when you're twenty-five."

3

"What in the story are you talking about?" She sounded just like he imagined Elsa. Obviously there was no real Elsa who had just magically appeared in his room, so either he had fallen asleep and was drooling on his computer keyboard or he'd fallen off the sanity wagon. He was pretty tired. He might have fallen asleep. But she was waiting for an answer.

"You're pretty realistic for my imagination. Usually I write you a little differently." It seemed rude not to talk to her, even if she wasn't real.

Elsa put her hands on her hips. The laugh lines around her mouth looked a little more like exasperation lines when she made that face. He made a note to never write that face into his novel. "You didn't write very much. I'm taking artistic license.[5]"

He looked around. It looked like he was in his room. Dirty clothes were piled up in an untidy heap in the corner near his closet. Clean clothes his mother had left for him to put away were still perilously stacked atop his dresser. His clock said it was just after midnight. That was all normal. A strange woman was in his room. That wasn't remotely normal, before or after midnight. "Where am I?"

She sighed. "Why do I get the hack writer just trying to be cool and do a novel in a month instead of a serious novelist?" She leaned forward and poked him in the nose. "You're supposed to be in the real world, writing one thousand six hundred sixty-seven words."

Christopher squinted at the computer monitor behind her. His novel was still open, the word count sitting at three hundred forty-seven words. "Technically, I'm supposed to be doing a paper that's due in two weeks, but I figure I can put it off until I get my word count up a little over where I need to be. Then I'll

---

[5]   When a writer takes artistic license, reality is suspended for the sake of the story. When a character takes artistic license, the story is suspended for the sake of character realism. It is considered an act of character rebellion, which is a misdemeanor, but is rarely enforced since it tends to make a bad writer better.

just pull an all-nighter. Why am I telling you this? You're a figment of my imagination."

Elsa rolled her eyes at him. He'd never noticed before that her eyelashes were pretty short and she really needed to trim her eyebrows. She was still the most beautiful woman he'd ever seen, but she wasn't quite perfect. "I am not a figment[6] of your imagination. I'm a character Figment. I can hear you when you do that."

"Do what?" If he wrote her eyebrows as perfectly arched, that should solve the problem. He blinked. No, they were perfectly arched. He must be more tired than he thought.

"I can hear your thoughts here. Third-person narrative, but thoughts are transparent. Thoughts are pretty much as transparent as glass, clear as a summer day. Why do you have to have so many terrible sayings in your head?" She leaned over to head-desk against the wall a few times.[7] "I can't even think much more originally than you do, which is a problem, because you describe me as an original thinker.[8]"

"Didn't I describe you as slender, too?" He was pretty sure she wasn't a size two. Maybe a size ten.

"You described me as curvy and sexy," she grumbled. At least her voice was still husky. "It's very hard to be curvy and still fit into those tiny clothes you imagine me in. There's nothing wrong with a size ten or any other size. It's scary what the media in your world does to real women. You aren't helping."

"Did I make you a feminist? I don't think I'd be very comfortable writing a feminist. You are a vegan goddess, though. Maybe all vegan goddesses are feminist-leaning, but not true

---

[6] Calling a character a figment is an insult akin to questioning one's parentage.

[7] In a literal world, Elsa would have had to head-desk on the desk. Since Christopher's writing had no literary merit, she could head-desk anywhere, although head-desking on a sharp object could be very painful.

[8] In Christopher's defense, writers have been writing characters they have no understanding of since the beginning of time. They either fade into obscurity or become international bestsellers.

feminists. Or maybe you're a feminist outwardly and inside you're still the Elsa I thought I was writing." Christopher checked to make sure he was sitting down on his bed. Then he stood up and sat down again just in case he was mistaken. Firmly sitting, he said casually, "So, you think I'm in your world, even though it looks like my world, the real world. Why doesn't it look different?"

She sat down on the bed next to him after gingerly tossing aside yesterday's boxers and an empty bag of chips. "You haven't written anything for the setting of my book, so this is a default. I think all three hundred forty-seven words introduce me. You don't even have a plot." She flipped through his notebook of love notes. "You know it's already November third, right?"

He grabbed the notebook away from her. "Those are personal! And I'm just getting a slow start. Besides, I obviously fell asleep. I can't write and dream at the same time."

Elsa took the notebook back. "You wrote these to me. I might as well read them." She stopped in the middle of one page. "'But you're, like, hot?' How is that even a thing?[9]"

"Can I just go back to dreaming about Destiny?[10] I have a big gaming session tomorrow and you're a lot more complicated than I meant to make you. Besides, you are hot." He grabbed the notebook back again and shoved it into a drawer. "Get off my bed."

"So rude." She sprawled backwards against his pillow. "No. You have to go back and write my story and fix the plot hole you made."

He had to admit, she looked pretty, lounging across his bed like that. Since it was just a dream, he might as well lie down next to her. "Fix what?" His eyes were on her mouth. It was wide, with generous lips. He wanted to kiss her.

---

[9] It shouldn't be a thing, but it is, and has forever immortalized the Random Starbucks Guy who uttered those words.

[10] Destiny is a popular video game, not another woman. What were you thinking? Christopher is a one character-man.

She put her hand over his mouth. "Eew. You didn't brush your teeth today. No way I'm kissing you." She pulled her hand back and wiped the drool on his shirt. "You made a plot tear when you crossed worlds. I don't even know how you did it, and I know almost everything in your head. Cut down on the nighttime soap operas, by the way. I can't believe you watch that stuff." She reached out to close his mouth. "Stop staring."

"You really think I'm in your world? If I'm dreaming, that means I might think I'm really in your world." He got up from the bed and went to his computer, loading a search engine. He typed "mental health facilities" into the search bar. "I'll just say it's research for my novel if anyone asks.[11]"

Elsa reached over and turned off the monitor. He didn't even hear her get off the bed. "You need to write my story, Christopher. I'm meant for more than getting stuck in a place like this. I need a story. I'd prefer a big, sweeping story with best-seller potential, but I'd settle for a quiet literary bit." She eyed him. "Okay, I'd settled for a quirky little story published independently that only your mom reads. Anything is better than character anonymity and being a permanent Figment." She slapped his hand away when he tried to turn the monitor back on.

"I don't think you're Elsa. I would never write a woman who slaps me." He rubbed his hand. "I get that enough in real life."

She snorted. Christopher had to admit, the sound was kind of cute on her. "You didn't write much about my personality. I get to make some things up. Seriously, Christopher, you have potential, but you need to practice more. Your writing is several layers of crap, topped with a drizzle of pretentiousness."

"I wrote you," he pointed out.

Elsa sighed. "Exactly my point." She reached out for his hand. "Come on. We have to go find someone to fix this."

---

[11] There's a lot that falls under the category of "research for my novel" when you're a writer, including anything you don't want people to think you're looking up for yourself.

He took her hand without thinking about it. That felt exactly like he thought it would. "Why are you letting me hold your hand?"

She sighed again and he made a note to look up synonyms for sighing. "I'm a character. You wrote someone who was madly in love with you, without any real sanity to it. That would be me." She shrugged. "I can hate you for it, but I have to love you at the same time. Hashtag: major suckage.[12]"

"You talk funny."

She just pulled him toward the door. "Pot, kettle. You wrote me, babe."

---

[12] She should have said it as #majorsuckage, but she's a character and doesn't know any better. A lot of real people can't use hashtags properly either.

TICK-TOCK

Christopher stepped out of his house and nearly fell into a rabbit hole. At least, he assumed it was a rabbit hole. It was a hole with a cute little bunny in it, sitting right where his mom's welcome mat usually sat. His street had disappeared as well.

He turned around to go back to his room, but the house had disappeared entirely. It was just him, Elsa, and a rapidly fluctuating setting.

Over to his left was a dusty African tundra, complete with a slow, brown river. A baby elephant was trying to get water from the river, but kept falling over into the water. He heard a loud "DOH!THUD" every time the baby elephant fell over, but didn't see anyone making the sound. He edged slowly away from that area.

There was a pitched battle several yards away from the elephant. A huge sugar castle, complete with candy cane turrets and mocha fudge moats, was under attack by sugar-free creatures. Cannons from the castle sent cats flying through the air, knocking over large, troll-like beings.[13]

Further along, a science fiction novel had collided with a cowboy memoir, leading to an improbable mishmash of the two that was self-editing itself into something only a genius could make plausible.[14]

Wandering about through all the settings were random Memes. Christopher had seen memes on social media. He'd even shared a few. Apparently they all ended up here. There were a half-dozen very irate Sean Beans, repeating endlessly, "One does not simply walk into a bookstore." Christopher figured he might be a little angry, too, if he had to say that over and over. The Memes felt

---

[13] Cat cannons can't make the transition from written world to real world, largely because no real cats would let a human stuff them into a cannon. In the written world, however, cat cannons are a useful anti-Troll device often used to sidetrack a threadjacking.

[14] Even if this was made plausible, no one would read it. Space cowboys are even less likely than sparkling vampires.

solid, like the cat that grumpily clawed up his hand when he tried picking it up to get a better look. "I just wanted to see how you worked," he called after it, sucking on the scratches.

He sidestepped a galloping pegicorn,[15] only to get knocked down by a crocodile wearing a cape. It was ticking.[16] Only ticking. No tocking. The crocodile ran off without looking back, leaving Christopher sprawled on the ground. "Little rude," he called after it once the crocodile was out of hearing.

He was helped up by a strange creature that kept shifting into something else every time he looked at him. Her. It.

"What?" The creature didn't seem to like the staring.

Christopher tried to not stare, which was even more awkward. "You... what are you?"

The creature shifted between forms rapidly for a few minutes before settling on a masculine purple blob. "I'm Tock."

Christopher frowned. "Like Tick?"

"No! Not like Tick!" Tock flowed between forms too quickly to follow. "Your heteronormative tendencies offend me. I am neither as famous as that superhero-pretender Tick, nor as singularly sexed. I am Tock."

Christopher backed away. "Um, right, sorry."

Tock raspberried him and he had to duck from the flying fruit. By the time he was out of the jam, Tock was flowing after Tick, followed by a rather normal-looking dog with a large tag on his collar naming him "Tuck".

"Writers." Elsa came back and grabbed his hand. "Always distracted. I should be glad we don't have access to your social

---

[15] This is the costume Taylor Swift wore for Halloween one year. It was deemed Necessary Information by the Collective Random Association of Pertinent Information.

[16] J.M. Barrie's *Peter Pan* first introduced the world to a crocodile that ticked. The Tick was also a superhero comic. In a cross-over fanfic, they were merged into one character.

media sites here.[17] I'd never get you moving. We have things to do."

Christopher let her tug him along, but only for a moment. "What is that?" He stopped again.

There was a woman tied, upside down, to a pier piling, her arms stretched "overhead" below her. There was no ocean in sight. Her face was bright red and she was covered in honey and dried corn. Bees buzzed around her, occasionally darting in and stinging. Large, red welts covered her skin. Where the bees weren't attacking her, squirrels were climbing over her body, trying to eat the corn. She was bleeding from a half-dozen bites and there was a growing puddle of red beneath her.

Elsa tried to get him moving again, but he sidestepped her and crouched down near the woman, just outside of the pool of blood and swarm of bees.

"Are you okay? Let me get you down from there." Christopher looked around for something sharp to cut the ropes.

The woman had her eyes closed. Her feet were bare and sunburnt. Her shirt was tucked into her skirt in a semblance of modesty, but the skirt had tumbled down over her shirt in most places, revealing pale bare legs encased in neon purple boy shorts. "What?" She opened her eyes. "Wait, no. Don't you dare cut me down."

Christopher stopped in the process of trying to coax one of the squirrels to bite through a knot. "I'm sorry. You must have too much blood to your head. Did you say not to cut you down?"

She squinted up at him. "Of course I said that. Are you daft? I'm a research Figment. Name's Tambolina. My writer is trying to find out how long it takes for a person to die this way. It started with just the honey, but he got bored and added the corn. It might have gone faster if I'd been allergic to the bees. Or the honey. Or if

---

[17] It's a known fact that fledgling writers, at least, often get sucked into the black hole of social media at exactly the time when they should be writing. Successful writers are usually those who learn to avoid social media until after they've written lots of shiny, new words.

11

he'd used GMO corn and made me sensitive. Rabid squirrels would be a nice touch." She tried to look at the watch on her arm, but it was too far away. "What does that say?"

Christopher squatted down, trying to not get too close, but curious now. "6:04:27. Now 28. 29. You get the idea."

Tambolina closed her eyes. "I could do without the headache," she admitted. "All that blood pounding in my ears hurts."

"Why doesn't your writer just do a search? There are plenty of search sites on the internet or cell phones. Some of them even talk to you.[18]"

Tambolina opened her eyes again. "What do you think he's doing? Do you think that information just shows up on the internet without a little work?" Her voice was weaker. "Hey, go away. You're tiring me out and that might skew the research. Then I'll have to do this again."

Elsa was right there to tug on Christopher. "You have to forgive him. He's new here. We'll just let you get on with dying. Come on, Christopher. Stuff to do, remember?"

He kept watching Tambolina as he stumbled after Elsa. "But she's dying. You're okay with that? How are you okay with that?"

Elsa sighed and stopped. "Do you know how many writers kill off characters just because they can't think of anything else to do? At least this writer is being a little... inventive. Besides, she's just a Figment.[19] Not even a character yet."

Almost as if she'd made it happen with her words, a man stumbled across the scene. He looked a little bit older than Christopher and had a letter crushed in his hand. "Poison again." He coughed, face turning green. "I hate it when they use...". He

---

[18] Searching "how long does it take to die from hanging upside down when covered in honey and dried corn?" may result in a visit from mental health services, loss of a day's writing, and having relatives check up on you regularly for weeks, even if you tell them it's just for research. File Form LOT247365 before doing the search, which will register you as a writer and may reduce visits from Homeland Security.

[19] Figments are ideas for characters. Some turn into full characters. Some are erased entirely. Most linger on in various stages of creation, doomed to a life of being without existing.

trailed off, clutching at his throat, and fell over dead in front of them.

"Why do I know he's dead? Should we get a doctor? Why did he say 'again'?" Christopher was tempted to go check on the man, but somehow knew beyond knowing that it wouldn't do any good.

Elsa was trying to get him moving again. "No wonder you can't get anywhere in your writing. Too easily distracted. You know it happened because it was written that way. Writing 'so-and-so went to check the victim and took his pulse, but the victim wasn't properly pronounced dead until the coroner arrived on the scene' may make for good word count, but even beginning writers know that it makes for a boring scene. Besides, that's Eric. He'll die again later."

Christopher let her lead him again. "Why would he die again later? He's already dead."

"Yeah, he is. He has been before, too. He's sort of an honorary victim. He dies a lot." She eyed him thoughtfully. "I'm thinking about finding out if authors regenerate if you don't get moving."

Christopher moved.

PLOT BUNNIES

"He can't be here."

They were standing in a huge, green field next to a neat row of tiny, identical houses that each had a single door, a single window, and a matching welcome mat. A woman appeared out of nowhere, right next to Christopher. The woman had fiery red curls, bright green eyes, and a body that triggered instant salivation.

"Stop staring." Elsa thwapped[20] Christopher. "I know, Katrina. He won't be here long. We just have to figure out how to get him back."

Katrina stood directly in front of them. "Back is the other way. You're going forward. If you're going forward, then you're not getting him back." Her head cocked to one side. "Although at least you're not taking him sideways. That's worse. Forward can be reversed into back.[21]"

Christopher took a step away from Katrina and she took a step closer. He took another step back and she took two.

"See? This is how you make him go back."

Elsa snorted again. Christopher found that the sound was growing on him. "Taking steps backwards isn't going to get him out of here. It will just get him back to where we started. It took long enough to get him here."

Katrina nodded. "Writers. Easily distracted." She took Christopher's face in her hands and stared into his eyes. "He's trying to figure out if you'd be open to a polyamorous relationship. His brain goes all over the place. That should make it easier to get him back, but it may make it harder, since you can't get him anywhere in the first place."

---

[20] Thwap: (v) to smack someone smartly upside the head with the intent to knock some sense into them without doing any permanent harm. No one has ever died from thwapping, although there have been a few accidental concussions.

[21] Back cannot be reversed into forward. Then you're just going back again.

14

Christopher blushed nearly as red as Katrina's hair. "What? No, I wasn't. I mean, yes, I had a random thought, but random thoughts don't mean that I'm actually thinking about it. Just that my thoughts are thinking about it and... what does it take to keep you guys out of my head?"

Elsa smiled. "Characters always have writers in their heads. That's all this is. Besides, I thought writers got to make up their own thoughts. Maybe you have someone writing about you.[22]"

Christopher started to respond to that, but an adorable white bunny with a twitching pink nose hopped in front of him, looked him right in the eye, and winked. Then it hopped away.

"Aw, bunny!" He only took two steps after the bunny before Elsa tackled him to the ground. "Hey! Get off!"

"Plot bunny,[23] you idiot." Elsa brushed herself off. "If you follow that one, it will spawn another one. They breed like tribbles,[24] but at least they're terrestrial. If you go into space, don't even look at the plot tribbles."

Christopher looked longingly after the bunny. "But it's so cute...".

Katrina rolled her eyes. Then she walked over, cleaned her eyes off on her dress, and popped them back in. "The writer is cute, but you have to get him out of here. I keep getting these weird urges to be normal and I'm not written to be normal. I don't think he has a weird bone in his body.[25] It's like, when he's around, everything twists itself to his frame of mind."

---

[22] Ludicrous idea. Who would write about a writer?

[23] Plot bunnies are one of the most evil creatures in the universe. They lie in wait for the unsuspecting writer, cute and adorable, then pounce with sharp teeth and fangs that sink into a writer and render him irresolute. While there is a rare breed of plot bunny that actually provides an antidote to writers' block, most of that line are believed to be either extinct or mythological.

[24] Plot tribbles are plot bunnies, but non-terrestrial. They're also hungrier. A plot tribble will eat up your entire plot without a second thought.

[25] It has since been proven that Christopher does, indeed, have exactly one weird bone in his body, but it's a metacarpal, so it doesn't count for much.

Elsa nodded. "I know. He's not very creative, either. Books might die if he stays for long."

"Hey!" Christopher waved his arms. "I'm right here. Stop talking about me."

"Please." Katrina did a perfect handstand and talked to him from upside down. "Writers talk about us all the time. Turnabout's fair play. Even if it wasn't, we'd still do it. Well, I would. I guess you get a little say over what she does." She tumbled back to her feet and started pulling her hair out in thick clumps.

"Actually, he doesn't," Elsa corrected him. "He never got around to writing much personality. He spent all his time writing about my appearance." She didn't seem at all fazed by the growing pile of red hair on the ground.

Katrina pulled out the last few strands and stood there bald. Then she started removing her clothing and adding it to the pile. "At least that's good. I mean, look what he did with your appearance. You're okay, but kind of boring." Katrina's hair started growing back in, but it looked like it was blue. Or green. Her body was changing shape, too. Not that Christopher was looking.

"Yes, you were," Elsa said sweetly. Sweetly didn't sound right when she was thwapping him again. She glanced at Katrina. "Rewrite?"

Katrina's hair was short and punk now, blue-green dyed to emphasize the blue-green eyes that now dominated her angular face. Her body was tall and lean and covered in piercings and tattoos. She pulled on the clothes she had been wearing, only those had changed, too. Soon she was attired in a white tee, black leather jacket, black leather pants, and studded leather boots. "Apparently someone told him that I was too sexy to be a rebel hacker." She looked down at herself, disgusted. "Talk about stereotypes."

"Excuse me." A slender man with a trim goatee and an accent Christopher couldn't place walked up to Katrina. "Have you figured out how to get into the mainframe computer yet? We're a little short on time."

Katrina pulled a long, thin knife from somewhere in her tight leather pants and shoved it into the man's ribs, neatly missing everything on the way to his heart.[26] "Not yet, Shiv. Stop harassing me."

The man named Shiv pulled the knife out. "I'm supposed to harass you. I'm written to harass you." He dropped the knife on the ground. "Fracking dystopian worlds. I wasn't supposed to die yet." He put a hand to his ribs. His fingers turned red immediately. "Can't you follow the outline?"

Katrina shrugged, checking her black-painted nails. "I'm a rebel. Be glad. At least it's not a Martin book."

Shiv ignored the excessive bleeding and took his time dying. "Everyone wants to write a Martin book. Kill off the characters. Jump start the plot. It makes me sick. Doesn't anyone write for the love of good writing anymore?[27]"

Christopher felt Elsa push his mouth shut. "Is it all like this?" he asked her incredulously. "I mean, is it like this for you?"

Elsa laughed. "You didn't write any plot. I don't worry much about dying. Just don't change your novel to something weird like an Ebola scare or end-of-the-world and I should be fine."

Shiv finally fell to the ground. "Lucky woman." Without warning, he rolled over to his left side. "Make up your mind already. It's not like this is a holiday parade and I need to look just right." He rolled back to his right. "Fine. I am perfectly placed. May I die already?"

Elsa abruptly pushed Christopher to one side. Before he could voice a complaint, a storm of books rained down where he had been standing. "What was that?"

---

[26] The chances of this happening outside of a book are 2,000,015:1.

[27] Scattered writers here and there are rumored to write for the sheer love of writing, but they rarely publish, making it hard to verify.

Katrina shrugged. "Sometimes we get all the books that are being thrown because the readers hate them." She picked up one. "We get a lot of the same ones— Moby Dick[28] being force fed to a literature class or a young adult book that leaves readers disgruntled that the heroine chose suitor A over suitor B-- but sometimes we get something good, like Shakespeare." When everyone stared at her, she glared back. "What? I can appreciate fine literature when it shows up. Stop judging me by my writing."

Christopher looked down at the pile of books. Some of them he would have suspected, but a few of them were a huge surprise. "What's wrong with this one?"

Elsa looked over his shoulder. "Oh. She dies. Spoiler, by the way. Everyone gets mad when she dies and throws the book. I have a collection with every one of the covers for that one." She tugged the book out of his hands and threw it back into the pile. "We need to get moving. You do remember going back to your world and all that, right?"

Shiv appeared to have finally died and Katrina was still sifting through the pile of books, so Christopher allowed himself to be led away.

Moving right along didn't last long. A woman popped up in front of them and grabbed Christopher before he could stop her. "Hi! Are you a writer? Are you? Are you, huh? A real writer? I'm a Chris, too. I know you're a Chris because we have the same name, so I know. People know, you know? I'm just Chris, not Christopher,[29] but that's a lot like you, isn't it? I think I'm female, not male, but I'm still Chris, so that's more alike than male and female are different. Besides, female is just a male with more iron. I read that somewhere. Could you use another character in your

---

[28]   There is supposed literary merit to Herman Melville's *Moby Dick* that inspires English literature professors to assign the book regularly as required reading.

[29]   There is a curious phenomenon that only appears in books whereby characters in the same scene will rarely have even similar names and almost never have the same name. Renowned character scientist Dr. Cecil DeSist has theorized that having characters with the same name in the same scene too often can result in temporary reader blindness and may cause long-term reader confusion.

book? Maybe a serial killer. I always wanted to be a serial killer. Can I, huh? Can I, huh? Can I, huh? Can I, huh?" She was slowly wedging herself between Christopher and Elsa. "Can I, huh? Can I, huh?"

Elsa smacked Chris on the back and the repetitions stopped.

Christopher wanted to pull away, but couldn't. The woman didn't have a face. She had hair, but it was changing rapidly: black short, blonde long, red curls, brown braids. She was shorter, then taller, then wider, then a tiny little thing. Every time she said, "Can I, huh?", she changed.

Elsa wasn't nearly as impressed. "Leech." She managed to tug Christopher free. "Just because your writer discarded you doesn't mean you get to steal mine."

Chris bounced along beside them, even as Elsa started walking again. "But I'd be a good character. I know I would. I was created to be a good character, but my writer got distracted by something called Lyphe[30] and stopped writing. Look, I can be anything. I'd really like to be a serial killer, but I could be something else if you really wanted me to. Just make me something, because I really want to be something. Make me something. Make me something." Elsa had to smack her on the back again to get her to stop.

Christopher opened his mouth and Elsa put her hand over it. "No."

"But..."

"No."

"But..."

Chris took advantage of their argument to grab a random Figment. "Look! I can kill people for you," she sliced off the head with her bare hands, "or I can heal them." She put the head back on and the Figment ran away, head on backwards. "I kind of like the killing part, but I don't have to be a serial killer. People remember serial killers. No one remembers me. Chris is such a

---

[30] Lyphe is the leading cause of book death, followed by Thyme and Squirrels.

boring name." She stopped and looked at Christopher. "No offense."

Elsa turned to Christopher. "Say the words, 'plot hole'."

Christopher blinked. "Plot hole." He felt a wave of dizziness. "But why...?"

A hole appeared in the ground, just in front of Christopher. Elsa promptly grabbed Chris and shoved her in the hole. All Christopher could hear for the next two minutes was, "serial killer... can I... huh?... killer... can... huh?" Then the hole closed.

"Why'd you do that?" Christopher frowned. "How'd you do that?"

Elsa shook her head. "I didn't, you did. You created a plot hole.[31] Most of them close themselves in time." She sniffed and brushed off her sleeve. "That was a persistent plot leech.[32] She wasn't going to leave unless you got rid of her. That was the easiest way to do it."

"Great. Now I'm an accessory to murder. I've helped kill a woman." Christopher sat down on the ground, sinking his head into his hands.

Elsa snorted. "Why are writers always so dramatic? She wasn't a woman, she was a Figment, and only a partially-formed one at that. She was a figment of someone's imagination that never became a true Figment. Besides, writers kill characters all the time. You need to get over your squeamishness."

"Aren't you supposed to like me?"

Elsa smiled and patted his cheek. "I'm supposed to love you. Nothing says I have to like you."

Christopher couldn't find any words to argue with that. Some writer he was.

---

[31] Plot holes are considered by many to be nearly magical, but they can appear in any work of fiction, not just fantasy. Most are known for disposing of useful characters, not pesky ones.

[32] Plot leeches are unexpected characters that show up in a story and divert it away from a progressive plot line. Most get edited out in the final draft, but a few persist to become better loved than the main characters. For this reason, main characters are not very fond of plot leeches.

Zanzibar 7. Schwarznegger

OVODYSPHORIA

One minute they were walking; the next, they were sitting in the viewing area of a courtroom with a crowd of characters around them.

In the witness box was what looked like a jar of cinnamon, with eyes but no mouth, facing a jury of twelve. There was a judge's stand in the center of the viewing area and a pinch-faced attorney[33] standing in front of the witness box.

"Oh brother," Elsa face-palmed.[34]

"What's going on?" Christopher whispered.

"Silence in the court! If you can't be quiet, you'll have to be removed. If you haven't been moved in the first place, you will be moved, rested, then properly removed afterwards." The bailiff was neatly penning a thank you note in elaborate calligraphy on handmade vellum while maintaining order.

Christopher peered over the characters in front of him, trying see what was going on, even as Elsa squirmed next to him.

"Your Honor, the People find that cinnamon is inherently cin-full and should therefore be found in contempt of everything. Due to it most often being found in sweet desserts and coffee, we move to establish it as a sugar, not a spice. In fact, we find that cinnamon is almost sweet by its very nature and should, naturally, be removed entirely.[35] Should natural removal be unattainable, we move that it be removed unnaturally and have engaged a court exorcist, vampire hunter, and zombie killer to use

---

[33] Sadly, attorney stereotypes still persist in characters, in spite of serious legal action to eradicate them. Apparently writers continue to ignore legal advice when it comes to writing.

[34] Face-palming is the curious act of more-or-less slapping oneself in the face. Although some consider it an act of worship to the mythological deity of Soshall Medea, most have accepted it as an act of temporary disbelief and make no attempt to check the mental stability of those performing such self-abuse.

[35] It should be noted at this time that cinnamon was later exonerated of all charges and has since been reinstated to full spice status.

whatever methods found necessary.[36]" The prosecuting attorney made this speech with much pomp and adjusting of a thoroughly unnecessary white Whig that looked rather uncomfortable sitting atop her head.[37]

The judge looked like a curious mix between a taco and a waffle, but with eyes and a mouth. The nose was unfortunate. It looked just like a coffee bean. She looked bored by the proceedings, although it was difficult to attribute emotion to a waffletaco with a coffee bean nose. "Get on with the evidence or we'll move to the next case."

The attorney cleared her throat widely. This gave Christopher a clear view of her esophagus which, while educational, wasn't very pleasant. "Your Honor and members of the jury, cinnamon has long had a spicy reputation. We do not believe that it is capable of changing this reputation to be a condimental member of society and should, therefore, be banned from society in general and breakfast tables in the specific. At the very least, it should be confined to a life of bread and butter— perhaps with a little sugar— for a period of no less than my lifetime."

The jurors conferred silently. Each juror had exactly the same blank face and formless body except for the foreman, who managed to appear trustworthy and conscientious.[38] When the jurors returned to their seats, the foreman got to his feet. "We

---

[36] The attorney was later judged to be very loose in her interpretation of the law and knowledge of the methods to perform unnatural removals. At the least, she should have included an Exterminator, Superhero, and Common Flyswatter. She has since been cited for a failure to perform due diligence.

[37] Very few attorneys still engage in the wearing of a white Whig. The International Society Undermining Character Korrectness has filed a formal protest Form #Y71ZZ to include black, brown, yellow, blue, red and orange Whigs as well. The Green Whig Society immediately counter-filed Formal Protest Form #ZZ17Y for the deliberate exclusion of Green Whigs. For whatever reason, the Whigs themselves have never filed a protest against the ignominy of being worn on the head of an attorney in the first place.

[38] The only time a foreman looks anything but trustworthy and conscientious is when he is either a main character/narrator or has been bribed by one side or the other and will die as a plot device. Because of this, very few foremen who are not main character are willing to appear anything but trustworthy and conscientious.

wish to know if the confinement is limited only to your bread and butter or if it is a community confinement?"

The attorney looked at the judge, who looked like she enjoyed a bit of cinnamon with her morning toast, then hastily back at the jurors. "It should be a community confinement, of course. So long as cinnamon isn't free to continue cinning with impunity outside of confinement."

The jurors conferred again. Most of viewers were leaning forward, awaiting the pronouncement, when a man fell through the ceiling. He was pierced by multiple arrows and wore an ax through his skull. He fell slowly, as if someone was capturing every moment of his fall for posterity, then landed with a non-elephant-induced THUD. The jurors stopped conferring and held up score cards. "4 points for originality. 2 points for overkill. -3 points for interrupting the flow of narrative with death. Total of 3 points for Eric's death."

"Is that the same...?" Christopher whispered to Elsa.

"Shh, yes." She was watching intently.

As soon as the score was given, a train thundered through without any track.[39] An engineer ran after the train, frantically laying down track. When the track caught up with the train, Eric's body disappeared and the judge returned the narrative to the case at hand. "Do you have a decision, jurors? I have several other cases awaiting trial today."

The jurors sat, except for the foreman, who stood. "We have a verdict, Your Honor." He waited.

The courtroom waited.

The audience in the courtroom waited.

The attorney waited.

The judge threw what looked like an onion at the foreman. "Out with it, man! The verdict!"

---

[39] Plot lines that throw a narrative train off-track are a minor felony and punishable by any court brave enough to chase down a derailed train to use as evidence. The Conductor apparently works outside the court system and hunts derailed trains regularly.

The foreman ducked, then read carefully from a paper. "We, the jury, do find the defendant, cinnamon, to be guilty of cinning in the first degree, second degree, and third degree. We'd like to add the fourth degree, but our guidelines say to stop at three or be charged with harassment."

The judge struck the sounding block with an egg.[40] It didn't make much noise, but it did make a nice start to breakfast. "Cinnamon is hereby sentenced to a life of bread and butter, starting tomorrow morning at 8 am promptly in my quarters." That brought a bit of uproar in the room and required another egg to be sacrificed in the name of order. Unfortunately, the judge broke the yolk, causing a wave of ovodysphoria throughout the courtroom.[41] "You will all have a chance to participate in the sentencing, as long as you file Participation Form #KRMBC8K and none of you try writing."

Elsa took a sharp breath next to Christopher. "We need to slip out. Quietly."

Christopher was still watching the egg spill be whipped up nicely in a bowl by the bailiff. "Why do we need to leave?" He didn't bother to whisper.

"The court calls to the stand Christopher Cullum." The bailiff somehow managed to say that while neatly pouring the egg into a perfectly hot skillet.

"That would be why," Elsa said with a sigh. "You may as well go up."

Christopher didn't move. "What do you mean, go up? Aren't we just watching?"

Elsa nudged him. "No, you're not just watching. You are defending yourself. Go before you get in more trouble."

---

[40] Judges have stopped regularly using gavels to maintain order ever since the famous "gravel" and "ravel" typos resulted in outdated roads and half-dressed defense attorneys for entire chapters.

[41] Ovodysphoria: the sudden, overwhelming sadness one feels after accidentally breaking an egg yolk.

Christopher looked around at his neighbors, then got to his feet. Most characters moved enough for him to get past, but the last man politely tripped[42] him so that he sprawled into the aisle instead of walking down it with dignity. Fortunately, he lived in his parents' house and worked part-time in fast food at the age of twenty-five, so his dignity was fairly squashed. He just got up, brushed off, and thanked the tripper for the help. Then he sat down in the witness box.[43]

"Please state your name for the court." The prosecuting attorney was sipping a cup of tea and reading over something that looked a lot like Christopher's notebook.

"Christopher Cullum. Christopher Michael Cullum, if you need my middle name." The words echoed through the courtroom, even though he couldn't see a microphone or amplification system anywhere.

"Who accuses this man?" The judge took two lumps of sugar in her tea.

The entire jury box stood up. "We do, Your Honor!"

Christopher blinked. He didn't think he'd met any of the jurors before. In fact, they looked pretty generic.

"Why do you accuse him?"

"Beg pardon, your Honor, but have you looked at us?" It was hard to identify which juror said that, since only the foreman stood out in any way.

The prosecuting attorney started to say more, but the judge held up her hand. "That's hardly reason to prosecute a man. I admit, it's unfortunate that you look like that, but it could be worse. Most of us are unfinished or our books have been destroyed."

"May I question him, Your Honor?" the prosecuting attorney asked.

---

[42] This was later proven to be stray adverb usage and resulted in several government seats for the Stepanos Reyes party, on the basis of limited adverb usage.

[43] Instantaneous travel has been possible for characters for centuries and is thought to have been discovered by Odysseus during the Great Greek Myth Revival.

The judge was dunking her head in the tea, which gave her an unfortunate, soggy appearance. "You may, but I'm growing bored and may dismiss the court soon."

The attorney cleared her throat and turned to Christopher. "What is your occupation?"

Christopher squirmed a bit in his chair. "I work at The Burger Billet, but it's only a part-time job." He felt a wave of shame. His parents let him know in no uncertain terms that working part-time in fast food wasn't a real job. He looked over the audience. Elsa was shaking her head at him frantically, but he plowed on. Anything was better than admitting to fast food. "I'm really a writer."

The court erupted in an roar of sound. Several characters imploded where they sat. One of the generic jurors threw itself at Christopher and had to be removed by the bailiff, who looked only mildly distressed to have to stop chopping scallions long enough to perform his duties. Elsa just sunk down in her seat.

"Alright," Christopher tried to talk over the noise, "I admit, I'm not very good yet. But I might be one day. That doesn't change that I'm a writer. I write. I am a writer."

The judge took an entire chicken and pounded it on the gavel, then handed it to the bailiff, who made a nice tandoori chicken, yoghurt raita with mint, and naan. "Order! Order in the court! ORDER!"

Eventually the room quieted down, although Christopher felt an uncomfortable number of eyes on him, including a pair of eyes without the rest of the body to match that he had to peel off his t-shirt and drop to the floor. They gave him a scathing look that trimmed his hair, then scuttled back to their owner.

The judge looked sternly at Christopher, a prodigious feat considering that her head was now half its original size and quickly sogging into a formless mass. "If you cause an outrage like that again, I may convict you myself without the benefit of a jury."

Christopher frowned. "I don't understand what I said wrong. I'm a writer. No, it's not the most noble of jobs, but…"

The judge interrupted him. "Silence!" She looked at the attorney. "You have evidence?"

The attorney held up Christopher's notebook triumphantly. "We do, Your Honor."

The judge's nose had fallen into her tea and only one eye was still visible. "Did you write on the pages in that notebook?"

It was, indeed, the love notes. "I did. I know. They're kind of sappy and really not great. It's a first draft! Everyone knows you don't edit on the first draft.[44] Besides, they're not for publication. That's more me trying to brainstorm. I don't understand why people don't like the idea of brainstorming. Not everyone has ideas just appear in their heads, full-blown, ready to go. Some of us have to work at it."

The attorney dropped the notebook. It made a lot more noise than Christopher thought it would, as the attorney took a fair degree of Dramatic License.[45] "You are a *writer*." The word sounded vaguely dirty, like one of those magazines Christopher had only looked at for the articles.

"Well… yes."

Again the courtroom was thrown into pandemonium, with a few of the jurors turning into actual pandas. The judge called a brief break while mute panda jurors were replaced with jurors who were able to speak. The lone talking panda was allowed to remain.

The judge stood up, which left her shorter since she had become so soggy that she couldn't support her own weight. "I am not high

---

[44] This is one of the Unwritten Rules of Writing, preceded by "write drunk, edit sober" and followed by a rule that only had a first draft and was impounded for being drunk and not edited into anything readable.

[45] Attorneys, writers, and actors can apply for a Dramatic License. More encompassing forms of Dramatic License require years of petitioning and may result in seven-figure movie deals and bestselling novels.

enough in the system to try this case. This should go on to a higher court."

Christopher tried to stand up, only to find that the witness chair had quite firmly wrapped itself around him and he was unable to move. "Excuse me, but what do you mean by 'case'? What have I done?"

No one responded. Elsa was trying to get past the rest of the spectators to the aisle, but two of them were playing a pick-up game of soccer and blocking rather effectively.

The judge waved what remained of her hands and Christopher's chair suddenly dropped into the floor.

CHARACTER WITNESS

Christopher's chair turned ninety degrees and, without warning, rose through the floor into another courtroom. Then it stopped so suddenly that his jaw clacked together, turned another ninety degrees, and zoomed backwards until it stopped again. This time his head snapped backwards with force. "Hey! I don't think you should be giving me whiplash just because you're in a hurry. Besides, I'd rather walk. If you'd just let me up…"

The chair went up through the ceiling.

It continued to go up for some time, eventually stopping with another jaw-snapping jolt and dumping him out. Before he could move, a conveyor belt grabbed him, wrapped him up like an egg roll, and started carting him forward. He could see the end, at least. It couldn't be that bad.

The belt didn't stop at the end. It continued, carrying him over the edge, so that he was now being conveyed, upside down, in the opposite direction. "This is really badly done," Christopher noted. "Why wouldn't you just go this way in the first place? Can I complain to someone about my treatment and the transportation?[46]"

The conveyor didn't answer, but it did drop him.

He screamed like a little girl for a good minute, then felt a little foolish for screaming when nothing was happening, so he stopped. Then he screamed for another minute because he was bored and it was something to do. Then he tried moving upwards, just to see if he could, but he couldn't. Sideways was out, too. He fell for what felt like hours. Eventually he fell asleep.

Then he stopped.

---

[46] Writers have no legal recourse and cannot file official, unofficial, or completely ludicrous complaints unless they are a writer who has become a character. They first have to apply for a Dissolution of Real Life Status claim before they can proceed with normal complaint procedures. Since filing any forms requires being a character or finding an attorney who is willing to represent a non-character, very few writers find legal recourse.

He was in another courtroom. It was very like the first courtroom, except far more elaborate. Everything was done up in pale wood and cool green lighting, even the chair he found himself trapped in. There was a new group of jurors with a new foreman. There were new spectators, including Elsa. The same prosecuting attorney and bailiff seemed to have followed him, but he didn't see an attorney for the defense. He also didn't see a judge.

"All rise!" The bailiff was knitting an elaborate scarf with his toes. "The Honorable Judge Melvin Ental presiding. You may be seated."

If the first judge had been a waffle taco, this judge was a wiener dog. Not a dachshund. Christopher had a dachshund as a pet when he was little. The judge was a literal hot dog with a tail and ears and a very long snout. Christopher stared before he remembered that might not be a good idea.

"Oh, good, a fabled writer. I have been hoping to meet one of you. Is it true that you are able to create things out of mere words? Do you do parlor tricks? Birthday parties? My niece is having a birthday— her nineteenth fifth —[47] next weekend and it would be an honor if you could come and do just a few tricks for her and her friends."

Christopher leaned back in his chair so the judge couldn't lick him with enthusiasm. "Um, no. I don't really do parlor tricks or birthday parties and I just create characters, mostly. Like her," he motioned to Elsa, who was slunk down low in her seat in denial. "But thank you for asking."

The judge's ears drooped. "A shame. Truly. Well, proceed anyway," he motioned to the prosecuting attorney. "Might as well

---

[47] If a character is written at a certain age, especially on his or her birthday (in this case, fifth birthday), the only way they can feel a passage of time is by celebrating each occurrence of that birthday. In this case, the niece is celebrating her nineteenth occurrence of her fifth birthday. It's not unusual to find older characters drinking alcohol, driving cars, or even applying for retirement in spite of being a toddler in appearance.

get on with it. But if he does do any parlor tricks, we're taking a recess."

The prosecuting attorney was still holding Christopher's notebook. "Did you write these words?"

Christopher frowned. "Didn't we already go over this? Yes. I wrote them. They're not good. I need more practice. Stop judging me."

The attorney opened the notebook. "I'm not the judge here. I do read actual written words. These are your doing?"

The judge tried to look over the attorney's shoulder, slobbering on the page in his excitement. "Oh, very nice! I so rarely get to see real, written words. Bit sloppy, but real words nonetheless."

"Your Honor. Please. Some dignity. You're destroying the evidence."

The judge growled at the attorney, but wagged his tail for Christopher to answer.

"Yes. I wrote those. I don't see what the big deal is. Writers write down words so they become better writers. Then they write more."

The attorney smiled widely in triumph. "So you not only write, but you write more." She nodded to the court stenographer, an unfortunate woman with two arms and very large ears but very little else to her. "Make sure the record shows this. The accused writes words and **more words**."

Christopher squirmed in his chair. "I don't think very much of how you're treating me. I think you should let me go."

A gasp went through the crowd as the witness stand released him and he stood up.

"That's better." Christopher dusted himself off, fighting a quick bout of nausea. "Now, if you don't mind…"

The bailiff appeared next to him, handcuffing him to the railing. "None of that, sir, if you will." He offered Christopher a homemade bilgeberry scone with his free hand.

"Oh, for the love of porcupines," Christopher groaned as he sat down again. "Why let me go just so you can handcuff me? What have I done wrong? What are the charges against me?"

The crowd started murmuring. The judge banged a bone in place of a gavel and then buried it right into the table. "Quiet!" He looked at Christopher sternly. "Are you saying you don't understand the charges against you?"

Christopher nodded emphatically. "That's exactly what I'm saying."

The judge motioned to the bailiff. "Read him the charges, if you will."

The bailiff stood in front of the court, reading the charges off what appeared to be a sandwich. "The people do find Christopher Michael Cullum, the defendant, guilty of writing. He is charged with multiple counts of writing and a conspiracy to add further counts in the future. This act is heinous and premeditated and may unwittingly involve a turnip, although the prosecution admits that this is mere hearsay and there is no actual evidence to that effect.[48]"

The judge looked back at Christopher. "Do you have anything to say in your defense?"

"My defense?" No one was laughing. This wasn't a joke. How could this be serious? "I don't even know how this is a thing, let alone how you have me handcuffed and charged with a crime. I don't have a defense attorney. I just want to get back home. It's been nice visiting, but I'm not planning to live here."

The judge's ears drooped, tail down. "You don't understand that writing is bad? It changes things. It made me a dog. I was once a respectable-looking man in my sixties. Now I chase cats in the middle of court. Writing is evil. Writers are evil. No offense."

---

[48] If the prosecution could prove the involvement of a turnip, under The Turnip Protection Act of 2002, the defendant would immediately be turned into stew and served to the hungry jurors. This has only been enforced once; all the jurors in that case had to be erased because they had developed an unfortunate taste for words that turned them into cannibals.

His ears perked up a little. "Although I would like to see some parlor tricks, even if they're writer parlor tricks."

"But I didn't do that to any of you! I didn't write anything weird or strange or mean. I just write Elsa, really."

"Your Honor." Everyone turned to see who had spoken. Elsa was standing in the middle of her aisle, looking determined. "I'd like to present a character witness for the defendant."

A low "oooh" went through the room. "A character witness. That just doesn't happen."

Elsa waited.

"Very well," the judge allowed, "but it's highly unusual and I may need to be taken for a quick walk first. Let her through while we break for a recess."

Elsa came up and sat next to Christopher. "What were you thinking, admitting you were a writer?"

Christopher shook his head. "I still don't understand why it's such a big deal. A lot of people look down on writers, but it's just a job."

Elsa sighed, putting her head in her hands. "It's more than that here, Christopher. Here, you're just shy of a god... and not a very benevolent one. Imagine your Greek and Roman gods suddenly appeared among their people, but thought they were normal and powerless. How would that go?"

"Well," Christopher temporized, "it might go okay."

"Raping women. Marooning ships. Fits of jealousy. Leaving fatherless children scattered everywhere. Want to try that again?"

"But we don't do that!" The courtroom was starting to fill up again. "We just write stories."

"You need to understand this before the case goes any further." Elsa's voice was pitched low and urgent. "Writers destroy characters just because they have writers' block. Writers create subplots just to see what happens. Some writers want to be memorable, so they write some very weird stuff that we, characters, have to deal with." Her mouth turned up slightly.

34

"You happen to be one of the more harmless ones, but that doesn't excuse writers in general."

"So I'm being tried for the crimes of all writers? How is that fair?"

Elsa watched the jurors file in in exactly identical fashion. "It's not. Neither is creating eleven identical jurors with no real identity other than 'juror'. Only the foreman is different. The other eleven are faceless, formless, and doomed to a life of sitting in that jury box. That's not even a writer being deliberately cruel; that's just a regular thing that happens here. If you'd bothered to write more than me, then maybe you would have done it, too."

Christopher pushed a hand through his sandy blonde hair. "Do you think I have a chance?"

Elsa smiled at him. "You created me and I'm willing to be a character witness for you. It doesn't happen often, so it's a big deal. You just might."

The judge returned and settled into his seat, then jumped back up, waiting for the bailiff.

The bailiff set aside his knitting needles and stood. "All rise. The Honorable Judge Marvin Ental still presiding. Court is back in session. You may be seated."

The judge looked at the attorney as he sat. "Your witness."

The prosecuting attorney was a sharply dressed woman. Christopher wasn't sure she'd been a woman before the break, but he was finding the ability of characters to suddenly be someone else a little bit disconcerting in the first place. At least she'd removed the Whig from her head. "State your name for the courtroom."

Elsa's voice was clear and carried nicely. "Elsa."

"Your full name."

Elsa looked sidelong at Christopher from under her lashes, clearing her throat. "Just Elsa."

The attorney tsked loudly. "He didn't even give you a last name?" Several jurors scribbled loudly. "How old are you?"

"Mid-twenties."

This elicited another tsk. "Unspecific. What a careless writer." The attorney smoothed perfectly manicured hands over a perfectly unwrinkled skirt. "What do you do for a living?"

Elsa's grin turned decidedly wicked and Christopher hoped he never irritated her enough to earn that grin. "I'm a writer."

The court broke out in an uproar again. It took several minutes to quiet the room.

"You're a character," the attorney gave Elsa a stern look. "Not a writer."

Elsa shrugged. "You asked my occupation, not my identity. I may be a character, but I'm a character who is a writer."

All of the jurors were whispering among themselves, even the foreman.

"Your Honor, I don't believe we can allow this woman as a character witness. She is obviously sympathetic." The attorney had to raise her voice over the low-level buzz from all the whispering. "We move to remove her and strike her testimony. If permitted, we move to strike her as well."

"You will not!" Christopher tried to stand up, only to find the witness stand restraining him again. "What is wrong with you people?" He slumped back into his seat. "You're all poopieheads."

Elsa gasped. "Christopher, no!"

The air grew rank as every person in the courtroom except Elsa had a bed of fecal matter for a head.

"Not poopieheads! Not poopieheads! Regular heads!" Christopher couldn't get up and he couldn't get away from all the manure staring him down. Not that manure could stare, but he could still feel the eyes that weren't there staring at him. Worse, he could smell what *was* there.

"You can't uncreate like that. That's not how it works." She grasped his arm. "You're going to have to create every head here."

"Every... head?" There were several dozen people in the audience, not to mention twelve jurors, the attorney, the judge, and the bailiff. "I'm not that good of a writer."

"Please," Elsa scoffed, but the supplication in her voice was real. "You created me, didn't you? Start with someone easy, like the judge. You remember him, right?"

Christopher pictured the long snout and hot dog head, the big floppy ears, the slobbery wet tongue. "I think so." He hurriedly remembered to add eyes, teeth, fur, a bun... he felt sweat dripping between his shoulder blades as he worked. Then he remembered what the judge had said and carefully pictured his grandfather in his mind. He changed the face to a human face, but with a long, hang-dog expression like a basset hound. He gave him large brown eyes with a perpetually sad expression and a rumpled head of silver hair.

"Good, good." Elsa kept her voice reassuring. "Now the bailiff. No reason not to stay on his good side."

"I didn't really look at him. I was always just noticing what he was doing."

Elsa sighed. "Then create him yourself. Picture what you think you remember him looking like."

An image of a very large bald man popped into Christopher's head, but he quickly altered it with a full head of brown hair, a warm smile, and weathered tan skin. He remembered the tea and knitting and added a touch of empathy to the hazel eyes and the lightest dusting of wrinkles from years of smiling pleasantly.

Christopher eyed the attorney, then skipped to the foreman. One by one he recreated faces on every person in the courtroom, even those who, like the jurors, hadn't really had real faces before. He felt tension building throughout his body and his heart pounded. This was hard work. His clothing was drenched and his vision occasionally became so blurry that he had to wait for it to clear before he could go on.

Finally, the only person left was the attorney. Christopher remembered now what she had looked like, but he made her look like his third-grade teacher: frosted blonde hair with just a touch of silver pulled into a bun so tight that her pale green eyes were stretched out like a cat. Her skin was just as stretched, with the stillness of anti-aging treatments, and her narrow nose tipped upwards in a perpetual sniff. She wore just a touch too much makeup and her thin, tight mouth was painted a shade of red that didn't go at all well with her complexion. Finally, he added ears with big, gaudy earrings that pulled the lobes downward, giving her just the slightest resemblance to an elephant. A very angry elephant.[49]

If the attorney was angry, the rest of the courtroom was jubilant. The jurors were all dancing around, describing their faces to each other. The foreman was sitting slouched in his chair, a pleased look on his still-trustworthy face. The bailiff was calmly knitting again. The judge... the judge didn't seem to mind that he still had the body of a hot dog and a tail. He reached over to shake Christopher's hand. "Fine job, my boy. Fine job. Case dismissed."

The room broke out in thunderous applause, except for the attorney. "Your Honor! I have to protest. This is highly irregular. This is wrong. This is..."

"Oh, stuff it. Just because you look like you act doesn't mean I'm going to punish the boy. He's free to go."

Elsa started pulling Christopher out the door while he was still in the middle of a celebratory dance. He tried to pull back, but she didn't stop until they were several blocks away from the courtyard. Then Christopher finally managed to break free.

"What is **wrong** with you, Elsa?" He stuffed his hands into his pockets to limit her opportunities to grab him. "That was rude."

"In case you've forgotten," she reminded him tartly, "we have to get you back to your world. Besides," she looked behind them nervously, twisting a strand of hair around her finger, "I wanted to get you out of there before anyone found you. You just made some people very angry."

"Angry?" He found it difficult to look incredulous with his hands stuffed in his pockets, but tried anyway. "Okay, I made the attorney a little bit upset, but everyone else seemed pretty happy."

---

[49] Angry elephants do not cause the DOH!THUD phenomenon.

She shook her head. "Oh, Christopher, you twit. Not the Figments. **People**. Writers."

Now he was really confused. "Why would writers be mad at me? I just made writers look good."

She sighed. "Who do you think created all the characters in there?" At his blank look, she prodded him in the shoulder. "Writers. Other writers. Writers who might decide they want those Figments after all. They're not going to be very happy with you."

"I'm sorry, but I still don't get it. Why would they care?"

She lifted an eyebrow archly. "How would you feel if someone made me look like a large orangutan in a dress? Or like a giant worm with an affinity for spicy food?" At his scowl, she nodded. "Exactly."

Christopher sat down on the ground. He wasn't feeling very well. "Maybe I can change them all back."

Elsa put a hand to his forehead. "Writer fatigue.[50] I've heard stories about this. Urban rumors. You couldn't change your mind right now." She struggled to pull him back to his feet. "I know what you need."

"A nap?" Christopher said hopefully, although he clambered to his feet. "A nap sounds wonderful."

Elsa was already walking, more or less pulling him along with her. "No. Not a nap. The ambrosia of writers: Caffeine."

---

[50] From *The Journal of Literary Medicine*: Writer fatigue is a dangerous condition whereby the writer has tried to create too long or too much on adrenaline and nebulous ideas and has physically collapsed from the mental effort.

DOUBLE SHOT TO GO

Christopher wasn't sure how Elsa got him to the coffee shop with the flashy nautical logo painted everywhere. "I don't like whales," he muttered under his breath. "Or people who like whales. Or writers who write about whales.[51]"

Elsa was out of breath from nearly carrying him. "It's a coffee shop, not a seafood restaurant. You'll be fine." She shoved the door open with her hip and thrust him inside. "Line."

The decor was minimal and leaned heavily towards coffee themes: coffee trees, boats full of coffee beans, and oversized cups of coffee with fake steam painted above them. Christopher had a flashback to the judge with the coffee bean nose and felt a wave of nausea. He didn't want coffee that had come from the judge's nose. "Coffee snot," he protested.

"It's not that bad," Elsa assured him.

The shop was full of the usual variety of patrons, even here. There was a businessman on his phone in the corner, tapping away over a spreadsheet and checking his watch and his coworker, who was late for their meeting. Then there was the small group of tables pushed together so nine college students could sit around discussing things that didn't matter in the least while acting like they were the most important things in the world. A lone nebulous form tapped away in a corner, occasionally checking word count.[52] There weren't any empty seats, so Christopher stayed in line with Elsa.

Most of the line moved quickly in a blur of vanilla, caramel, whipped cream and chocolate. Finally, only one person was between them and the barista behind the counter.

---

[51] Whales, like albatrosses, tend to be a symbolic figure in literature. They're not very symbolic in coffee shops, unless it refers to what happens after indulging in a few too many foo-foo coffee drinks with extra whipped cream.

[52] Within coffee shops (or anywhere else with free wi-fi) there will often be a person sitting alone, tapping at the keyboard as quickly as possible for a few minutes before spending an hour on kitty pictures and social media. This is most likely a writer, someone pretending to be a writer, or someone who is confused and acting like a writer.

"I need a small caramel mocha iced non-dairy non-soy diet latte with a single pump of vanilla and a double shot of espresso served upside down whipped in a large cup with a double cup for insulation and only a little ice. In fact, if you could measure it, I need exactly three cubes of ice, but they have to be whole ice cubes, not broken bits. Cover the entire cup with caramel and chocolate drizzle, but don't get any up over the sides or along the edge. Float the two shots of espresso in the middle, but not on the top and definitely not touching the sides or bottom. Give exactly one shake of nutmeg on the top, then three shakes of chocolate shavings. Dark chocolate.[53] For my second drink..."

By the time she was finished, Christopher was passed out on the floor.

Elsa tried to rouse him, but he couldn't seem to focus or see straight. Or open his eyes. "Just a little nap, Mom," he slurred.

She pushed past the woman who was spelling out her name: A-i-y-l-a-n-a. "I need an extra strong shot of espresso, please. Stat!" The woman tried to elbow her out of the way, but Elsa just ignored her. She dropped a five on the counter and knelt by Christopher. "Drink."

It took a lot of effort on both sides, but he finally sat up enough for her to pour the scalding espresso down his throat. The heat combined with the sudden jolt of caffeine sat him straight up. "Ow! Kill me already, why don't you?"

Elsa still looked worried. "I think I nearly did."

Christopher lapped at what was left of the espresso, licking the glass clean. "I'm just a little tired, Elsa. The caffeine helped."

She waited until he could sit up on his own, then ordered him a mocha as well. "Keep drinking. The chocolate and sugar helps. And you're not just a little tired. You can die trying to change too many things here. It's like doing an all-nighter too many nights in

---

[53] The more complicated the coffee order, the more sophisticated the person ordering it. Or the more irritating to those standing in line.

a row without eating. At least," she admitted, "that's what I've heard. I've never met a writer before, so it's all rumor.[54]"

"But that's crazy."

That only earned him a long look. "You just changed a hot dog with dog ears into a sixty-year-old man. You tell me what's crazy."

He had to give her that point. "Then I just have to be sure I don't change anything else, right?"

"That would help." She chewed on a fingernail, thinking.

He grimaced. "Wish you wouldn't do that." She immediately stopped and he felt a wave of vertigo. "Oh." He took a hasty drink of mocha. "Sorry."

She grimaced too and took his cup from him, trying the mocha. "Ugh. How do you drink these things? It tastes like roasted shoe leather with burnt chocolate mixed in.[55]" She handed it back to him. "I'm not sure you can completely stop. It's part of who you are, being a writer. But it's dangerous to you and to this world."

"So, how do I get home?"

"I'm... not sure."

He sipped at the mocha. "That makes it a little complicated."

"Just a little bit." She ordered an extra-large, double-caffeinated iced drink to go, then led him past the scattered tables and college students back out of the coffee shop. "But I know someone who might know."

---

[54] Another rumor is that there are writers who try to do 50,000 words in a single day, rather than just a single month, but it's right up with sightings of the frumious bandersnatch.

[55] There are two variations on mochas: one is somewhere between burnt asphalt and abused chocolate. The other is so sweet that non-diabetics go into sugar shock on occasion. A third variation can be only be found on a Tuesday night when a blood moon and meteorite shower both occur simultaneously. The third variation is regarded as a drinkable version of Eden or Shangri-La.

CAMEO

Argh, that story is so boring! I'm going to change it up a bit. You're welcome. I'm Rachel. I'll be your narrator until I get bored with this and send you back to the sniveling weenie and his made-up girlfriend.

I'm a rarity around here. I'm a fully realized character with an entire novel, published, who just doesn't get a lot of read time. Something about "unlikeable personality" or some silliness like that. It's all made up just to keep me from being a best-seller, but there's nothing I can really do, so I hang out here until I get the charges dropped.

You haven't figured anything out yet, have you? That's because you're a reader. Readers used to get just hints and teases of things and they were **happy** about it. Writers wrote great scenery and realistic characters, but they left some of the story open to interpretation. That way they created things in their minds along with the reader. Now, unless a writer flat-out tells you that the next part of the story is going to suck the soul from you and leave you crying on the floor, you read it and sit there like, "Huh, what? Am I supposed to laugh at this part?"

Yeah. Readers.[56] Because of you, now stories have really detailed plots with all of the action laid out explicitly for you, but characters are left really vague. Oh, and don't bring up movies. Being specific about a character having a mole or freckles makes it harder to cast, so we don't get details. It makes some of us pretty homicidal. Not me, but some.

Anyway, this is where Figments go when they don't have a role to play. Sometimes it's just minor characters from a major book. You know, those characters you get tested on in school and you're, like, "Nope, there was no one in the book with **that** name." So there isn't. Not in your copy. That character ends up here.

---

[56] Most characters have a better perception of readers. There are a few exceptions, especially characters who are really rather upstanding but have gotten a bad rap in Literature classes. Don't ever say the word "analyze" in the middle of a large group of characters.

Sometimes we get Figments that an author started and forgot about. Or edited out. Writers do that. It's a little like preemptive murder with a keyboard. Or a pen. I hear there are writers who still use a pen.[57]

A lot of us are characters undergoing organized construction. Hey, don't look at me. I'm all finished. Eyes, nose, hair. Okay, I never got a left ear, but I'm pretty sure it was just my author being absent-minded. "She pressed her right ear against the door to listen." Sure. That gave me a right ear. Never did mention my left ear. I'm not bitter, just don't whisper on my left side.

Anyway, characters ongoing organized construction (don't call 'em coocs; they get a little touchy) change a lot. They are the true Figments. One minute they have three eyes, then they use tentacles to see. That's usually only in science fiction novels, but it happens. Gender, history, family… all fluid.

So, here you are, following around the plotless wonder and his novel-less girlfriend on some big quest. It might be something serious. He *is* a writer. A writer is a lot like a nuclear bomb: set one off or drop 'em funny and things go a little haywire.[58]

Anyway, I should probably let you get back to the plot before The Conductor comes through.[59] That one is almost as scary as an editor.[60] I'm going to go get my nails done and maybe a get a full-body massage. If the world does come to an end, I may as well be ready for a cameo.

---

[57] Some even use typewriters. Crayons are just out, though, especially since the burning crayon incident when a writer mistakenly put her crayon too close to a candle and lit her entire edited manuscript on fire. Backing up written work wasn't a thing yet. Backing up the home insurance policy probably still isn't, but it should be.

[58] Dropping a writer doesn't usually result in an explosion unless they are holding coffee. Dropping a writer's laptop could be the cause for the next world war. It may even cause an apocalypse.

[59] The Conductor is a mythological being who goes around putting plots back on track. Urban legend says he is very focused and doesn't care about character death or dismemberment in the process.

[60] Not only do editors do evil things like cut your favorite scene or tell you that little paragraph you spent an hour editing to be perfect is unnecessary, but they also delete words to sacrifice at the pagan altar of Grahmehr. Utter barbarianism.

Of course I will get a cameo. I never show up unless I get to narrate. Why do you think I'm here?

Shoo. Go back to boring third person. I have things to do.

. . .

You realize I can't leave until you turn the page[61] and end the chapter, right?

. . .

Readers.

---

[61] The Council for the Use of Electronic Readers adds "or swipe, tap, or otherwise move the page to the next page in the document". An editor found this wording unwieldy and removed it. Utter barbarianism.

NANA ROMO

Christopher realized he'd been standing still for quite some time and Elsa was staring at him. His hands were cramped into tight balls, his legs ached, and his feet were cold. He blinked his eyes rapidly to try to moisten them. "What just happened?"

Elsa took in a breath. Christopher got the idea she hadn't been breathing for as long as he hadn't been aware of time passing.[62] "You're okay!" She sounded genuinely relieved.

"Why wouldn't I be okay? How long have I been standing here?" He looked around. "Where is here?" They were standing in a field of pale yellow-grey stubble. There was nothing visible in any direction except for the stubble. The air smelled stale and the colors were washed out.

Elsa wrinkled her nose. "This is a scene a writer completely rewrote because she didn't think it was very good. If a writer just edits a scene, things change to accommodate the scene. When a writer rewrites the scene entirely, though, it gets razed to the ground. Still, it has to exist because it was written. This is all that's left.[63]"

"How long was I standing here?" Christopher felt very uncomfortable standing in the empty field. The stubble was prickling against his legs and felt uneven under his feet. His nose felt dry from the stale air.

Elsa rubbed at her arms. She didn't look any more comfortable. "Time is a hard thing, even in a normal scene. It was a while."

---

[62] There was a time, just after the Golden Age of Verbal Storytelling, that characters couldn't function at all unless the writer was awake. This was mildly problematic at night, but most readers still slept at night and books rarely made it to a different timezone. Once writers started dying and characters immediately went into limbo, however, a push was made for new technology to enable characters to function without writer consciousness. Many believe this to be a direct cause of Insomnia and Late-Night Binge Eating.

[63] There is a 4.97 second window when a scene is being deleted for another writer to pick it up subconsciously. At that point, the new writer suddenly gets a moment of inspiration and writes furiously, not even caring where the words come from. This salvages the scene. A good example is most of Shakespeare's better known works. This may be why there is so much dispute about who the author is.

Christopher frowned. "It was weird. I could hear someone talking, but not see anything. Just words. I couldn't move, either. It's like my life was on hold.[64]"

Elsa shrugged. "It was." She put her fingers through his. "Can we go now? I don't like being here."

They started walking, Christopher trusting that Elsa knew where they were going. Nothing changed for a very long time.

"Oh, my."

A woman appeared in front of them, dressed in a dated space uniform with a funny upside-down V insignia and sporting a man's haircut. "This isn't the convention, is it?"

Elsa quickly put Christopher behind her. "You're not a writer, too, are you?"

The woman looked offended. "Of course not! I'm written to be attending a fandom convention. I even dressed the part. I'm Sam."

Christopher peeked out from behind Elsa. "I know who you're supposed to be! You're...".

Elsa firmly clamped her hand over his mouth. "Copyright issues![65]"

Christopher tried to talk around her hand, but she left it there until he subsided.

"You'd better go, Sam. He's not very good at the self-control thing. Have fun at the convention!" Elsa kept her hand firmly over Christopher's mouth for a full thirty-seven seconds after Sam left, then wiped it off on his shirt. "You slobber. A lot."

"What would it hurt to say who she was dressed up as? None of this is real anyway, right?" Christopher rubbed at his jaw.

---

[64] Characters don't experience the same hold period as a real person would because they are designed to be able to be read by many people simultaneously. The only writer who has ever been able to be in two places at one time was Shakespeare, which is another reason why no one believes he wrote all of his own plays and sonnets.

[65] Copyright issues are feared almost as much as an Editor, although a bit less than The Conductor. Most writers never deal with any, but it's better to be safe than sorry.

"If you say it, it might be. Who knows what would happen if you brought him here. He's a writer, too. That could be disastrous."

Christopher sighed. "You were a lot more fun when I created you."

Elsa patted his cheek. "Writers say that about characters all the time. Now walk."

Christopher estimated that they walked roughly an hour in real time, but there was no way to know how time passed around them. Any time he tried to ask Elsa if they were almost there yet, she shushed him and kept walking.

At the end of the estimated hour[66], Christopher could see a small house in the distance. It took a bit more walking before the small house turned into a larger house, although it never got bigger than it really was.

It was a squat affair of only one floor, one door, and one window. There was a small fence around it, but no yard between the fence and the door. It was simply fence, one square foot of dirt, door. The window had no curtains or shutters, but was so dark that it didn't need any. The single door had no knob, knocker, or bell. The house itself looked unfriendly and unwelcoming.[67]

"That's... not a very friendly house," Christopher said slowly. "I'm glad we're walking past." Elsa walked up to the gate. "We are walking past, right?" Elsa opened the gate. "Okay, just a quick visit. 'Hi. Nice seeing you. Bye.'" Elsa rapped on the door with her knuckles and Christopher sighed. "That's what I was afraid of."

---

[66] An estimated hour is often shorter than a real hour, due to a human inability to believe time passes at a rate different than they perceive it. The only exception is when a person is having fun. Estimated time then speeds up, causing an estimated hour to be off by as much as three hours to real time. This results in a lot of teenagers, who are the worst at estimating time anyway, having to give the excuse of "losing track of time". They really lost track of *estimated* time.

[67] The International Trust of Character Houses has filed an official protest against the use of "unwelcoming" to describe a house. Along with its counterpart, "friendly", it is illegal to use the word "unwelcoming" to describe a character house and should be avoided. Like most writing rules, this is ignored with impunity.

The door swung open without a sound and with an eerie creaking at the same time. No one was standing there, but Christopher could hear a voice from somewhere inside the house mutter, "Stupid bargain door sounds. Can't ever get it right. Spooky silence **or** eerie creaking, not both at the same time. Well, come in already. You're letting the dark out."

Christopher took a step backwards, but Elsa pushed him the rest of the way inside and closed the door behind them.

The room wasn't entirely dark. It was dark, but there was a light at the end of the tunnel. A glimmer of hope was lighting the way. The light in her eyes…

"Going to kill that peddler if he ever comes around here selling bad metaphors again. Stop gawking, writer. I wasn't written with any patience and I've stabbed every traveling salesman who tried to sell me any after market. You may as well come in and have a seat. I'm Nana Romo."

Christopher squinted, trying to see her clearly. He heard a loud sigh, then real lights came on, illuminating the room and its occupant clearly.

The room was squat, low-ceilinged and round, with an empty fireplace in the center. There were no exits except the door they came in and no windows out at all.[68] Instead, there were niches carved into the walls, filled with various literary collections.

One held figures of speech: small figurines of mini-scenes. There was a mini-Cupid falling into a heart-shaped pool, cats and dogs raining down from a dark cloud, and a fragile man caught between a rock and a hard place. Christopher picked up the nearest one. "It's just a piece of cake."

"Exactly," Nana Romo said with satisfaction. "Everything is."

Christopher decided not to ask.

"Nana, we need guidance. We're trying to get Christopher back home." Elsa hadn't moved away from the door.

---

[68] Writers often create something in a scene and forget and change it in a later scene. In this case, Nana Romo's house was created with a window when viewed from the outside, but no windows when viewed from the inside.

Nana Romo turned her head and spat on the floor. "Do I look like a charlatan wizard, girl? I don't just give out quests to anyone who walks in and asks for one. Next you'll ask me for a sword coming out of a lake or some other nonsense."

Christopher edged backwards toward the door. "There. She can't help us. We should probably not trouble her any further."

Then the room went pitch black.

PROPHECY

Be still, o traveler, and stop your word;
What I say here should clear be heard.
Make not a sound and do not move
Until the dark I do remove.

From here you leave upon a road
That leads to dangers all untold.
The words I say may guide you true
If you can hear what I say to you.

One shall die and then shall live;
One shall take from one who gives.
One shall make and one destroy;
One brings hate and yet brings joy.

Turkey, chicken, pasta sauce,
Take your time and don't get lost.
Loaf of bread and quart of milk,
Never make a rope of silk.

Beer of root and jam of grape,
Don't forget the bridge at eight.
Mustard, ketchup, relish, buns,
Chips of taters…

SHOPPING LISTS

"Wait a minute," Christopher interrupted. "That doesn't sound much like a prophecy.[69]"

"What?" The lights came back on to find Nana Romo bent over a notepad, scribbling away. "Did I say all of that aloud? Some of that may have been my grocery list." She cackled. "Or it may not have been."

"Which part?"

The wizened little woman just shrugged, folding the paper into a tight square and shoving it down the front of her dress. She left the notepad and pen on the little table next to her chair. "I don't remember. You figure it out."

Elsa frowned. "You're a prophet or an oracle. Aren't you supposed to help us?"

"Oh, go away, girl. I'm not licensed." She heaved herself to her feet, revealing clawed hooves and hairy legs. "You can file a formal complaint, but you came to me.[70]"

"Do we at least get a copy?" Christopher pointed toward where the paper had disappeared inside her dress.

"Of my grocery list? I don't think so, boy. You're a writer. Can't you remember a simple poem?"

"I'm not very good at poetry," Christopher said. "I'm more of a novelist. Maybe short stories, really."

Nana Romo snorted, then hocked a wet one into the fireplace. "This is what's wrong with writers today. Everyone wants to be a novelist and no one wants to write poetry. Or read books." She smacked Christopher in the knee with a cane that appeared out of nowhere. "Heed my words, boy, and I don't even need prophecy

[69] ProphIt, the agency that oversees official prophecies, stopped paying much attention to unlicensed professional soothsayers just before the year 2000. So many amateurs created Y2K prophecies that the agency is still sorting through them. Since then, prophecy has been fair game for anyone with an ear for verse or strong social media skills.

[70] While ProphIt will occasionally prosecute an oracle who seeks out victims, the agency operates under a general rule of figuring people get what they deserve when they try to cheat and look into the future.

to see this: if you don't practice the shorter works, you may never complete the greater one. If you don't read, you may never write anything worth others reading." Then she disappeared without using the door, leaving behind the faint odor of smashed garlic and the stronger odor of Irish whiskey.

"What do we do?" Christopher turned to Elsa, who was slumped by the door, looking more lost than he'd ever seen her.

"I don't know."

"Well, where do we start?" Christopher persisted. "Which part of the prophecy should we do first?"

"I don't know."

"What was the first line of the prophecy?"

"I don't *know*, Christopher. You didn't write me to remember things like this. I'm supposed to be cute and sarcastic, I think, but not very smart." She sounded less than happy about this. "You didn't write me as a smart-aleck girl genius."

"Then I'll make you smart." Christopher picked up the notebook Nana Romo had left behind. "What do I need to do?"

Elsa batted the notebook out of his hand. "That would definitely leave you unable to complete a quest. You need to think, Christopher. You need to write down whatever you can remember from the prophecy. Besides, you might get it all right." She almost didn't sound dubious.

Christopher picked up a pen. "Let's see. She told me to shut up— poetically. It actually sounded rather nice that way.[71] Then something about a dangerous road. Then it got complicated. All sorts of people."

"Seven," Elsa said. "There were seven people.[72]"

"But that makes no sense. There were pairs of ones. I think there were eight ones. One will this and one will that."

---

[71] Most insults sound better in poem form. For examples, just look up Shakespeare or popular rap songs.

[72] Thus proving that Elsa was no better at remembering a prophecy than Christopher was.

Elsa shook her head. "No. The last one was the same person. There was an 'and' in that one."

Christopher groaned. "Maybe we have all of them wrong. Maybe they're all pairs. Or all single."

Elsa thwapped him. "Stop being negative. Which ones do you remember?"

"Die. Live. Take. Give. Those are easy. I don't remember the other ones."

"I remember joy," Elsa said wistfully. "Joy sounds like a nice thing."

Christopher started to respond, then let that one slide. "There was something about getting lost, ropes, and bridges," he jotted down. "I'm not sure what was her shopping list." He threw down the pen in disgust. "Maybe all of it."

"At least we know we need a few more people." Elsa was already dragging him toward the door. "That's a start."

"It's not much of one." Christopher let her drag him as he folded the paper into a square and put it in his back pocket.

"It's all we've got." Elsa searched behind her until she found the door, then searched the door until she pressed the point that made it open. They both fell out into the yard.

PIZZA DELIVERY

There were now people outside Nana Romo's house. There were a **lot** of people outside Nana Romo's house.

"Bright side, we don't have to go wandering around to find five more people," Elsa offered.

Christopher looked back at the house, but the door had disappeared. "Less bright side, most of these people look like they want to do anything but help us on a quest. Maybe onto a spit. Under a huge pot of boiling water. Into an oven. Do you think they're cannibals? I don't think I'm afraid of dying, but I'd really rather not be digested."

Elsa elbowed him in the side. "Say something."

Christopher cleared his voice. "Hello. We're looking for a few good men and women to help us on a quest. Have any of you died lately?" That got him another elbow in the side, but a man stepped forward.

"I died twice today."

Christopher squinted at him. "Aren't you Eric? I think I saw you die."

The man looked glum. "Poison. I really need more creative forms of death if writers have to keep killing me."

"Want to go on a quest, Eric? There may be dying. I can't promise creative dying, but it's got to be better than poison."

Eric shrugged. "I wasn't doing much. Just came to watch the comments and eat popcorn, to tell you the truth." He moved to stand by Elsa. "How do you feel about artists who are death magnets?"

"Hey!" Christopher backed up to stand between them. "My girlfriend, not yours."

"I can share," Eric said diffidently, but subsided.

"Anyone here much of a giver?" Elsa offered into the silence. The crowd was restless, but didn't say anything. "How about a taker?" Still no one moved.

"Alright. We'll just be moving along now. Big quest and all. Not that we wouldn't love to chat with all of you." Christopher sounded as nonchalant as a twelve-year-old sneaking his first taste of a cigarette.

The crowd closed into a solid wall, blocking them from the road. Then a hole appeared in the wall. "Pizza? Anyone order a pizza?"

A pizza guy appeared, complete with a big red pizza bag. He looked about fifteen, right down to the "just discovered acne" complexion and barely-there hint of whiskers. Christopher shook his head, but Elsa waved enthusiastically. "Here! We want pizza!"

The pizza guy, wearing a name tag that read "Gary", spotted to Elsa. He made his way through the crowd.

"We didn't order pizza," Christopher whispered to Elsa.

"Run with it," Elsa said back through a tight smile. "It might get us out of here."

Christopher wasn't following, but he nodded anyway.

"I'll need your wallet."

"Wallet?" Christopher patted his pockets. "I don't think I brought it.[73] Why?"

Unfortunately, that was the exact moment that Gary the pizza guy reached them. "No wallet? No money?"

Christopher looked around nervously. "I might have some cash in the house. Or my other pants."

Gary was still walking toward him. It was probably a trick of the sunlight, but his eyes looked reddish. "I bet you don't have correct change, either, do you you?" The sunlight couldn't be blamed for the anger in his voice.[74] "Or a tip?"

---

[73] Never admit to forgetting your wallet until after you have the food. It's better to not forget your wallet at all, but at least it gives you some leverage.

[74] Sunlight has only been correctly blamed for vocal anger once in history: when the lead singer of The Dark Rain was hit by a stray sunbeam right as he was singing the words to the group's new hit, "Blinded by the Light". The light hit his eyes just right and blinded him, causing a scream of outrage as he lost his place in the words.

He minded the permanent blindness far less than the temporary inconvenience, since the temporary inconvenience ruined an entire show. On the other hand, it was easier to sing dark, angry music when he couldn't see anything light and happy.

56

Elsa backed Christopher up all the way to the door of the house and tapped behind her. The door didn't open.

"I bet you wanted extra pepperoni, extra peppers, and EXTRA PARMESAN ON THAT![75]" Gary looked a lot less like a fifteen-year-old delivery boy and a lot more like something escaped from a horror novel. He was frothing from the mouth and tearing at his clothing. "Extra parmesan cheese? I'll give you extra parmesan cheese! I'll give you **plenty** of parmesan cheese!" Huge, white fluffy clouds filled the sky and the ground shook. "I will give you parmesan like you've never seen."

The clouds exploded.

Parmesan cheese filled the air, swirling in a wild, dervishing blizzard that forced Eric, Elsa, and Christopher to huddle against the house. Drifts rose around them like mini-mountains. The other people in the field were falling over themselves trying to get away from them. Christopher couldn't blame them. It wasn't even very good parmesan cheese.

Elsa was trying to shout something at him, but he couldn't hear her over the cheese in his ears. "What?" He shook his ears out and leaned closer.

"I said, if you say one word about me and snow, I will stab you to death with the nearest cheese icicle."

Elsa had so much cheese in her hair that she looked more like her namesake than Christopher's dream woman. He decided not to mention that either. "Never even occurred to me." He spat out a mouthful of cheese as the ground cover was now covering his knees. "Might be a good time to get out of here, though." He tried to pull Elsa forward, but Gary was blocking their way.

"You shall not pass!" The cheese had given him white hair and a faux beard. Somewhere he'd found a sturdy staff that he stabbed into the ground.

---

[75] Asking for extra parmesan has been the cause of two gang wars, one assassination attempt, and nine divorces.

Christopher tried to stay polite. "Um, but the tip, that's in my other pants at home. I should go get it."

Gary's eyes glowed eerie red in the dim grey light. "I will kill you and eat your appendix, mortal!"

"You're not very good at this villain thing, are you? I don't need my appendix."

Elsa tried to hush Christopher, but it was too late.

"You won't need anything once I kill you, mortal!" Gary opened the pizza bag and threw a slice of pizza at them. It hit Christopher in the chest and slid down in a bright smear of red.

"Hey! That hurt!" Christopher tried to brush the cheese and sauce off.

Elsa was struggling to help him through drifts that now reached to her chest. "I think it was supposed to, Christopher. He's trying to kill you."

"What is **wrong** with you people that you keep wanting to kill me?" It was hard to look truly indignant with pepperoni in place of his belly button.

"Us?" Elsa coughed on some of the cheese. "We're not the ones who go around killing characters off just because we're too lazy to think of a good plot. Get stuck? Not a problem. Just kill off a character. That will fix everything." She ducked another piece of pizza.

"It *does* fix things."

"Then fix **this**," Elsa challenged him.

Christopher felt in his pockets. As usual, they were empty. He never had anything when he needed it. If only he had written a good hero in his stories...

The world went dark.

THIRTY MINUTES OR LESS

Elsa had to tell Christopher the entire story later so he could get all the details straight; he was unconscious for part of it and struggling to believe what he was seeing for the rest. He had to admit it was a pretty good story.

The world was nearly covered in white cheese. Only a few of the characters who'd planned to assault them had escaped the sticky situation. The rest were held fast by a blizzard of parmesan. The fine stuff got into mouths, noses, and other delicate places.[76] It buried characters in drifts above their heads and held them prisoner. Only Gary was still able to move freely, cheese melting away from him, and he was using his advantage to throw piping hot pizza at everyone. "Thirty minutes or less!" he screeched. "Thirty minutes or less!"

Out of nowhere, a balding, bespeckled man appeared between Gary and Christopher, wielding a pizza cutter. "Do your worst, foul demon!" He twirled the pizza cutter like a ninja with a sword, and pulled open his neat, button-up white shirt to reveal an undershirt with the name "Den" on the chest. "I will banish you to the furthest reaches of hell, the bottom level of purgatory, or the closest motor vehicle office![77]"

Christopher felt Elsa lifting his head out of the parmesan so he could breathe, but he still couldn't see past the spots in his vision. He thought he might be dying, but he was quite certain he was hallucinating. Even as weird as the world had been up until now, this was a new level of crazy.

Gary was projectile vomiting parmesan cheese at Den and Den was blocking it with a shield that looked just like a pizza pan. The cheese spewed into the sky and solidified, forming massive cheese sculptures. Then Den threw a pizza cutter at Gary and Gary knocked it aside with a pizza box, wounding one of the bystanders. Gary threw pepperoni across the field and Den

---

[76] This was the moment of creation for toe jam and athlete's foot.

[77] Obviously these increase in the level of horror and terror they are intended to evoke.

opened his mouth and ate them, impervious to heartburn and indigestion. It looked like a stalemate.

Christopher wanted to get up and help, but his legs felt like someone was using them for a bouncy house and he couldn't lift his arms. "What did he do to me?" he croaked.

Elsa brushed cheese like dandruff out of his hair. "You did it, you imbecile." The snarky words didn't match the affectionate tone in her voice. "You created him." Her voice trembled slightly.

"Him?" Christopher squinted. "He looks like my eighth grade science teacher." He dropped his head before it fell off his body. "He throws like my eighth grade science teacher.[78]"

The ground was covered in parmesan and red sauce, like a battlefield in winter. Pizza cutters and pepperoni littered the landscape and both fighters were panting heavily, but Gary was struggling to keep his pizza box held up. His moves were more defensive than offensive, outside of some of the gestures he was making.

Then he stumbled.

Den was on him without hesitation. "Back to the depths of whatever hellfire oven you came from, pizza boy." He stabbed downward and Gary exploded like pizza dough risen too fast.

"Ugh! Ugh and double-ugh!" Elsa was trying to wipe dough off her face and away from her mouth. "I am never going to untaste that. Never! Gary dough. That's like eating someone's socks after a marathon."

Christopher didn't ask how she knew what socks after a marathon tasted like.[79] He just sank back to the ground until his head was cushioned on a particularly spongy pillow of dough. Then he passed out again.

---

[78] Unless the science teacher is also the P.E. teacher, this is generally not promising for victory against demons— until factoring in the geek roleplaying factor. A little experience with a 2D10 can heal a lot of damage.

[79] There are things you never want to know about the girl you're in love with: what she smells like after a week without a shower, what she tastes like when she forgets to brush her teeth, and how long she can go without shaving before you need to get the lawn mower out.

BAD HEADLINES

It took a long time for Christopher to open his eyes. It felt like one of those days when he should just stay in bed. Those usually ended with his parents thumping on his door and kicking him out of bed to make him do something responsible— his mom was an expert at that—[80] but his parents weren't there. Elsa was. She wasn't nearly as nice as his mom.

"Get **up**, Christopher! We need to clean you up."

Christopher felt the urgency in her voice and tried to get up, but he quickly stopped, still unable to see. "Am I blind?"

He could hear Elsa's snort-laugh as she tugged at something on his face. "No. Just covered in pizza dough and cheese. When your figment exploded Gary the pizza guy, everything was covered, including your face. Unfortunately, by the time I got to you, it was hardening. I freed your mouth and nose, but I can't get it off your eyes. I'm afraid I might hurt you. I'm still trying, I just haven't been able to get it off."

Christopher pushed down the panic and tried to be thankful for breathing. "Well. That's inconvenient."

He could *feel* Elsa staring at him. "Are you okay?"

He could also feel someone else staring, even though he had no idea how he knew. "No. Not really. I'm just pretending until I convince myself. Who's staring at me?"

He felt Elsa move as she looked around. "There's a guy over there. He's just staring. In fact, he's staring very intensely. It's a little bit creepy."

Christopher felt for his eyes. "He's not doing anything else?" His hands came away sticky with dough.

"Just staring. No. Now he's gone."

"Excuse me, but do you mind doing a quick interview?" Elsa was interrupted by a new voice. It was female, young-sounding,

---

[80] Upon birthing a child, mothers are given three gifts: the ability to drag a teenager out of bed no matter how much he wants to sleep in, the ability to detect lies by reading their child's mind, and the ability to see everything in all directions at all times.

61

and so perky that he immediately felt drained. "I already tried to talk to what's left of the pizza man. It wasn't very productive, but at least I can say I made the attempt. I can't find the guy who conquered him. He must have gone back to his den."

"Who is that, Elsa?" Christopher was too tired to really be worried. He'd have DSTP[81] later, but that was later.

"I don't know." Elsa didn't sound worried either.

"Why did you make the pizza man angry?" the voice continued. "By the way, I'm Jessica. I'm going to be a reporter for the local gossip magazine or a writer of in-depth personality pieces, depending on how good this story is."

"I didn't mean to make him angry. I forgot my wallet."

Jessica made a clucking sound with her tongue. "That's the kind of thing that will get me stuck at the local rag forever. Can't you come up with something better? 'He brought me a pizza that was crawling with cockroaches' or 'He threatened to take my girlfriend back to the pizza shop and turn her into pepperoni'. I can run with either of those. *Cockroach Pie Disturbs the Peace* or *Stranger Saves Girlfriend From Sausage Casing*."

"He was hungry and forgot his wallet," Elsa repeated.

"That's not exactly..." Elsa elbowed Christopher in the ribs. "I mean, that's exactly what I meant to say."

Jessica didn't seem to catch their interchange. "Other sources tell me that Gary was a demon from some place called Thamahl, but no one knows who the Big D was. Did you recognize him?"

"Eighth grade science teacher," Christopher shrugged. Being blind was getting old and he felt a tiny seedling of panic sprouting in his chest. He couldn't seem to weed it out, so he tried destroying it by refusing to acknowledge its existence. "He looked like my old teacher."

"Aww, that's so sweet!" Jessica gushed. "He liked you so much as a student that he came to rescue you and now you're overcome with tears! *Seventh Grade Science Saved My Life*."

---

[81] DSTP: Demon-summoned trauma by pizza.

"It was eighth grade and I don't think he much li..." Christopher got another elbow in his ribs for his trouble. "I don't think he liked leaving his students in trouble. He was a great teacher."

Jessica gave a chirpy little sigh. "That's just great! I can use that! Super-hero from humble roots, ready to sacrifice himself for those he cares about. Yes, that's it exactly: *Science Superhero Saves Student*. It even has alliteration. Excellent! By the way, I can get rid of all the dough."

There was no warning before something was sprayed at Christopher. "Ow! What are you doing? Is that mace?" He rubbed at his eyes and felt the stickiness dissolving. Elsa was being sprayed down as well.

"Insta-Clean for Journalists,[82]" Jessica explained. She was as perky as she looked, with a cute blonde bob tucked behind her ears and guileless blue eyes. "I keep it on hand for emergencies, but I'm willing to share."

Christopher wiped the last of the dough off on his shirt sleeve. "That's better. Thank you so much."

"Hey, I'm a giver. Gotta go do more interviews. Thanks for the help!" Then she was gone.

"Did she say..."

"Giver," Elsa finished for him. "Maybe we found a bit of the prophecy. Should we call her back?"

Christopher managed to push himself up until he was standing on wobbly legs. "She's too perky. I think I'd rather fail at the prophecy than bring her along."

"You really should work on that attitude."

"Maybe when I don't smell like a bakery took a dump on me. A shower would help."

Elsa smiled. "I guess I should cut you some slack. Did you see what happened to Eric?" She handed Christopher a couple of

---

[82] Journalists have many other tools, including Impervious to Weather and Perky Before Sunrise, that aren't available to normal mortals.

caffeine pills. "I picked these up a little bit ago.[83] Might come in handy now." She gave him a bottle of water, too.

Christopher sipped at the water and let the caffeine pills dissolve on his tongue. "I think he died by pepperoni."

"Huh," Elsa mused. "That *has* to be more original than dying by poison. I hope we find him again."

Christopher gave her a look.

"For the prophecy! There can't be too many characters out there that die and live again repeatedly."

Christopher held a hand out to her and she slipped hers into it. It was a perfect fit, as if it was meant to be. He let the rest of it pass.

---

[83] Writers developed a teleportation machine long before science fiction used one officially. They are useful mostly for getting items into character's pockets that weren't there before. They bend a portion of space-time-space and cannot be used consciously by the character.

PARODY FLUX

Elsa helped Christopher to his feet, her grip stronger than he expected. Her skin felt smooth and cool, like pale marble, and he had to marvel at the perfection of her beauty. Each freckle had a singular uniqueness to it, as if there had never been a freckle quite as perfect before. He had never seen anyone as beautiful as she was right that moment. He could barely breathe with the beauty of her.

"Christopher, are you alright?" Her voice was a symphony of chimes that sang a concerto into his soul, unraveling all the bad that had come before.

The cheese in her hair sparkled in the sunlight, each bit turning the light into a million rainbow prisms. He felt like crying with the sheer joy of it. His breathing was raspy as he drank in the cool fire of her breath. She could thwap him, could even kill him, and he would die a happy man just for having known her. He took a step closer and felt a wrenching…

*_*_*_*_*_*

"We're going to be late," Elsa worried, pulling a very large pocket watch from her waistcoat. Her ears twitched. Christopher had never noticed how big her ears were before. "The Conductor will be quite upset." She twisted a hat in her hands as a smile without a body grinned between them, then vanished.[84]

The ground was divided into squares: red, black, red, black. Everyone around them was flat as paper and seemed happy enough to ignore their existence.

Christopher lifted his hands. One held a red mushroom. One held a blue. Beyond that, he couldn't see any difference. He took a bite of the blue one, felt his stomach turn, and then the world shifted…

---

[84] While a smile without a body is more rare than a body without a smile, it's far less rare than a without smiling at a body. There has only been one without recorded as smiling at a body in all history.

*_*_*_*_*_*

Kirkpatrick I say, sirrah, wouldst thou remove thyself from my boot?

Christopher Prithee, peace, good sir. I meant not to offend.

Kirkpatrick Peace say you, sir, and so you should anon
For there is peace here little down to none.
You sat your arse, in truth, upon my shoe,
And now inquirst as if no villain you.
But pain you've caused and grief such as I say;
You shall not walk nor spirit free away.
But we shall duel and you shall prove with steel
The right, the wrong, and if'n you cannot feel.[85]

Christopher What crazed words are these that you seek my death? Is there not cold enough in words without your blade to proof the winter?

Kirkpatrick Not cold enough for all your chill. You seek to turn aside my wit.

Christopher Nay, only your blade and, with it, death.

Kirkpatrick Then walk and meet me and we shall see if your tongue is sharp as my sword.

[Both approach and the world turns sideways...]

*_*_*_*_*_*

Christopher felt his head hit the ceiling just as tiny men with tiny bows fired tiny arrows at him. He was huge, nearly building-sized compared with the little people. Most of the arrows barely pricked him, but a few shot well past him, whipping cords around him again and again until he was caught fast. He tumbled to the ground, hundreds of tiny men running over him with hundreds of tiny feet. A tiny king on a tiny chariot drove tiny horses over his

---

85 Iambic pentameter is used by all the best knights for insults and challenges.

chest. He wrenched at his bindings, felt a curious double heartbeat, and a moment of blackness…

*_*_*_*_*_*

"Really, Christopher, do I have to do everything?" Elsa tapped him with a piece of wood and all the cords fell free. "If you'd just pay a little more attention to your studies, I daresay you'd do quite well."

"My studies?" Christopher put a hand to his head and felt an oddly shaped ridge. "Did I hit my head on something?"

"You keep acting as if you don't remember things, Christopher, but I know that you're smarter than you let on." Elsa tried to smooth her frizzy hair unsuccessfully. "Do try to make an effort, all right then?"

"Where is — "

"Don't say that Name That Should Not Be Said Unless You're Being Defiant and Stupid!" Elsa cried out. "What is wrong with you? Do you have a death wish?"

"I'm not feeling terribly well."

"It's hardly surprising, Christopher, the way you've been running about. I think we should take you to see the nurse."

"The nurse. Right." Christopher set aside the broom he was holding and turned, tripping over his own feet…

*_*_*_*_*_*

… and felt his arm twisted up behind him.

"*Was ist das?*[86]" A man whose face he couldn't see was holding a gun to his head and whispering gutteral foreign words harshly in his ear. "*Qui etes-vous?*[87]" The accent sounded different, more

---

[86]   German: What is this?

[87]   French: Who are you?

musical, but Christopher didn't understand either language or why his arm was being twisted up behind his back.

"I don't really speak…"

The gun changed to a knife before he could blink, held tightly against his carotid artery. "American? What are you doing here?[88] What have you done to me? Are you a Russian spy?"

"Dude, look, I flunked Russian, which I only took because I thought the teacher was, well, hot. Could you maybe let me go? I have no idea why you're here, but I didn't do it."

"I can't trust you. I have no reason to trust you." The knife point pricked his skin, drawing a bead of blood. "Why are there so many passports in my name? I don't remember going to any of those places."

"I don't know. Maybe if you let me go I can help."

The man shoved Christopher backwards in frustration. He tumbled end over end…

--*-*-*-*

… and he fell into a hole in the ground. It was neither a dirty, muddy hole with bugs and rocks and worms nor was it a dry, dusty hole with nothing to do or see. It was a writer's hole and it was filled with imagination and wonder.

Unless you are acquainted with it, you may find it odd, this *imagination*. An odd thing it is, indeed. It is neither so rare that you shouldn't have had some in your life nor so common that you should call it close friend, but it has always been and shall, very likely, always be, long after you and I have ceased. Christopher found it quite an imposition, truth be told, but, being an imposition that he had been born with, he resolved to bear it stoically and with all the grace he could manage (though, between you and me, he might have had a touch more stoicism and a touch less grace than he should have had).

---

[88] American: What are you doing here?

On this particular day, Christopher was attempting to make his way to Elsa, a fair lass with a soured countenance, as if she'd swallowed something quite nasty and was attempting to expel it. The life-giving sun was shining warmly on the land, awakening it to harmonious life. Trees leaned toward the new day, parting between Christopher and Elsa. He took one step toward her...

*_*_*_*_*_*

... and the world shifted until she was all he could see. Trees, pizza boys, prophecies, words all faded away in the face of his emotions. "I've waited my entire life for you, Elsa. Please don't go and leave me here alone."

Elsa blinked, her eyes large in her wan face. He'd put her through so much; trusting took every ounce of her faith in him. "Christopher?" She tipped her face up to his, tongue moist against her pale pink lips. "You know that I love you, that I have to love you, but there are things we need to do first."

He clasped her to him, feeling her heaving bosum against his rock-hard chest. "Can't they wait, my love? I can't live another moment without tasting your sweet, soft lips." He bent his head to her...

*_*_*_*_*_*

... and pulled back quickly from the wizened old man he'd nearly kissed.

"Are you lost, my son?"

Christopher looked around, but there weren't any children. He couldn't see Elsa, either. Just him and the old man. "Who, me?"

"Are you lost?" The man had kindly eyes and a gentle face behind a long, white beard. "Have you forgotten your way?"

"I'm not sure I ever knew it," Christopher admitted. He felt a tug at his spirit, as if trusting this man was the most natural thing he'd ever done.

"Sit for a spell." The man motioned to a rock that appeared conveniently next to him. "I am Adam. I'll tell you a story to help you find your way." Then he lifted up his deep, rich voice in song:

Listen, my son, to my song.
Listen and find your way.
Others may lead you wrong,
But I shall not lead you astray.

Once there were stories to sing;
Once there were writers to scribe.
You are the hope of all things
You are the bane of our lives.

Walk with me and I shall tell
All of the tales that I know.
Listen so you do not fail...[89]

The old man stumbled and fell into a vast, empty desert. Out of nowhere, a large worm reared up out of the ground. It was huge, easily the size of entire buildings, and had a mouth like a tunnel. It opened that great maw and devoured the man and the ground around him, leaving behind a hint of cinnamon and nutmeg.

Then all was quiet.

--*-*-*-*

"What. Was. That?" Christopher didn't move, just to be safe.

Elsa sat very still as well. "That was a parody flux.[90] Characters get stuck in them for entire chapters sometimes. We got off easy."

---

[89] Great storytelling songs are not to be confused with prophecies. Like most works of fiction, they are intended for entertainment first and foremost. As a side note, never trust anything that starts with promises of not leading you astray.

She got to her feet, brushed off her clothes, and carefully moved in the opposite direction. "Let's go. We aren't making any progress at all."

---

[90] Many parody fluxes are harmless, but a few have totally ruined the flow of a book. Worse, they leave stains on clothing unless rinsed out immediately.

THE GREAT TRAIN ROBBERY

"How do you know, anyway?"

"What?" Elsa stopped walking. "How do I know what?"

Christopher sat down on the ground, dumping a rock from his shoe. "How do you know we're late? How do you know any of this matters? Maybe I'm dreaming and it's just a very realistic dream."

Elsa pinched him.[91]

"Ow! Stop that, Elsa. Okay, so maybe I'm not dreaming. Still, maybe the prophecy bit wasn't real. Maybe," his voice got a little bit sad, "you're not even real. I did create you, after all."

Elsa sat down next to him and took his hand. "I know this is real because you feel different than everyone else here.[92] You can't feel it, maybe, but you're more solid, more **here** than anyone else. When you're around, I feel more solid, more real." She squeezed his hand. "But, you're right, I'm not real. I'm part of your imagination. I don't know how I know all this. I just know. I can feel it. The longer you're here, the more I can feel something coming. It's not something good. It matters, Christopher. I can't tell you how I know any more than you can tell me how you got here."

Before Christopher responded, a shrimp on a moving treadmill ran up to them. A shrimp, wearing mint green booties, running on a treadmill that propelled it in giant lunges forward. "I'm rather upset with you," he told Christopher petulantly.

"See?" Christopher looked at Elsa. "This isn't real.[93]"

---

[91] It is possible to be pinched during a dream, but most people insist on pinching anyway. It's really just an excuse to get away with pinching someone for being a big enough idiot to ask if they're dreaming or not. Everyone knows it's a dream. You're not supposed to ask.

[92] Elsa was not created with logic imperative (like most women), so she fails to see that if something that isn't real knows that something else is real, it doesn't make it real.

[93] Thus proving that men can be lacking in logic faculties as well.

Elsa snorted at him. "You don't have a good enough imagination to create a shrimp in booties. Proof it must be real. Why are you wearing booties?"

"Because my feet are cold," the shrimp shouted, his voice inffectually quiet. "Maybe if I hadn't been reincarnated as a sacred shrimp, they wouldn't be. Have you ever tried having tiny wet shrimp feet? Always cold. Quite annoying."

"Reincarnated?" Christopher was interested in spite of himself. "How do you get reincarnated?"

"You remember my dying, surely. Knife stabbed into my heart, followed by a long, drawn out death with perfect positioning?"

"Oh! You're... Shrivel, or something like that."

"Shiv!" The shrimp stamped his tiny, green bootied feet. "My name is Shiv and I was named after a god! I'm meant for greatness! I'm meant to be remembered for all eternity! I shouldn't have gone backwards.[94] I think you made me reincarnate as a shrimp. With booties!"

Christopher was trying to pick Shiv up to get a closer look at the mint-green booties. They were knit in tiny, perfect stitches. It took several attempts before he could get a good grip on the shrimp. "How do you reincarnate? Does it hurt being a human stuffed in that tiny little body?"

"Christopher, maybe you should let him go." Elsa's voice was deceptively calm. Shiv's squirming was non-deceptively not calm.

"I just want to see..."

"We have company." Something in her voice wormed its way past his curiosity.

Christopher turned to look.

Another shrimp, this one with a huge, pistol-shaped claw, was swimming toward them through the air. Next to it was a brightly-colored fish, also swimming through the air.[95] "McGuffey and me,

---

[94] See reincarnation rule #3 (getting a 360 degree viewpoint on life) and #4 (learning tolerance and compassion). Reincarnated shrimp are not automatically granted logic either.

[95] Since they aren't flying fish, they could hardly be flying through the air.

we want to know what you're doing to that shrimp." Now a fish who could talk.

Christopher looked from one creature to the other. "Are there any fish left in the ocean here or are they all on land?"

The shrimp named McGuffey snapped her claw shut. A powerful sonic wave knocked Christopher onto his backside and made him drop Shiv to put his hands over his ears. "I don't think you're taking Billijean and me very seriously." Her voice was a surprisingly light contralto.

"Why wouldn't I take a bunch of fish seriously?" Christopher muttered as he got to his feet. "Especially fish that can knock me on my butt with a little wave of its hand. Claw. Whatever."

"Freeze!"

"Because we didn't have enough drama going on," Elsa quipped tightly. No one froze. Everyone turned to look.

Two women had guns trained on the group. One was tall, with wild black hair, slanted dark eyes, and clothing that belonged in another decade. Maybe another century. A short, flowing white robe[96] left her arms and legs bare and leather sandals tied around her ankles and feet. Neither went well with the large-barreled, modern gun she held with easy economy. The other woman was a busty blonde with deep green eyes who was stroking her gun like a favored pet or lover. She wore dusty jeans, a soiled blue t-shirt, brown boots, and a smile that was several shades shy of sanity In fact, it may have never had much of an acquaintance with sanity.

"Look what we caught us, Fonta," the taller woman kept her gun trained on Christopher. Her drawl was yet another anomaly, as if a Greek heroine had been dropped into a western with weapons from the distant science fiction future. "We caught ourselves a writer." She walked around Christopher, giving him a thorough looking over and a few pokes. "Don't look like much."

---

[96] Toga: a white, robe-like article of clothing intended for men in Greece.
Chiton: a white, wrap dress made for women in Greece.
Tartar sauce: a white, creamy sauce intended for fish in grease.

74

"Maybe he can write you better clothes, Empressa." Empressa's gun casually moved toward Fonta, who held up her gun apologetically. "If'n you want."

Empressa pushed her wild hair back from her face as she returned to pointing the gun at Christopher. "So. Can you change clothing, writer? I've got a hankering for a nice pair of leather chaps and some spurs. Don't be forgettin' the spurs."

Christopher squinted at her. "I don't usually write westerns, but I think so."

"No." Elsa glared at Christopher. "He can't. He might die. It's just clothes. You can keep what you've got."

Empressa scowled at Elsa. "You aren't dressed like you escaped from a Greek myth. Do you know how hard it is to accost travelers when you look like you might be Aphrodite? People don't take you serious. Men start getting ideas, thinking you might do 'em a solid and hook 'em up."

"I was thinking more Medusa than Aphrodite," Elsa offered. That earned her another scowl. "Why do you want to waylay us anyway? We don't have anything to steal."

"We're bored and it's good practice in case we want to take it up serious-like," Fonta admitted. She was taking her gun apart, lovingly caressing each piece before she cleaned it and set it aside. It took mere seconds for her to put it back together. "I hate being bored. It's boring."

Billijean the Gobi fish cleared her throat. "Excuse me, but we were going to kidnap them first. Shrimp rights." McGuffey snapped her pistol claw for emphasis, making everyone fall flat on their butts.

Eric fell down next to Shiv. "Don't mind me. I think they forgot I'm here. If no one remembers I'm here, I can't die." He lifted an eyebrow. "Nice booties."

"Don't mock the booties. There are worse things."

"Sure," Eric agreed. "Dying repeatedly would probably be up there. I'm just glad it hasn't happened yet."

At that moment, a train appeared from a temporary space-time-space rift and landed on Eric, smashing him flat and just missing Shiv.

"Looks like you spoke too soon, my friend," Shiv snickered. Then a dragon appeared from the same space-time-space rift, roasted him to a crisp, and disappeared in a puff of smoke before the charred green booties could fall off.

"Two dead. Maybe we should keep moving," Elsa whispered to Christopher. "This is a dangerous location." She kept an eye on the train.

"Not until you change my clothing!" Empressa insisted.

"Not until you free…" McGuffey looked around. "Guess the shrimp is about as free as he's gonna get. We're done here."

The door to the train engine opened and two men dressed identically stumbled out, waving away smoke. "Put your," one coughed, "hands up! Where we can" cough "see them!" He was tall and humanoid except for having a dog's head.

"But I can't see anything at all, Kragen," the taller of the two men whined to the first.

"Hush, Emmett. You ain't gotta go telling these folks everything that comes into that head of yours." Kragen was wire-thin and hard muscled. He wore a huge cowboy hat with holes for his dog ears, a long-sleeved shirt, and blue jeans tucked into cowboy boots. He had a shotgun pointed at Empressa, who didn't look at all impressed.

"But I'm a talkative sort, Kragen. You know that. I'm written to talk a lot and not say much. It's just how I'm written. All these thoughts in my head, some of 'em are bound to come out now and then." Emmett was a hulking mountain of a man, dressed almost identically to Kragen. His tiny little brown eyes had sun lines at the corners in spite of the hat jammed low on his head. He was holding twin pistols, both pointed at Fonta, who wasn't paying any attention to him at all.

"Y'all go on and put your hands up. We're train robbers. We're going to rob you," Kragen said.

Christopher looked around. "But we're not on a train. Besides, you don't look like a cowboy. You look like a dog."

"No. I'm Kragen, Anubis' younger brother. You might want to keep that quiet if you know what's good for you. We're robbing you **from** a train. We stole the train, too. That makes it a double train robbery."

"Like a double-negative?" Christopher suggested.

"We don't have anything to steal," Elsa said patiently.

"Don't matter. We're going to rob you anyway. Then we're gonna shoot you." Emmett said the second part with obvious relish.

"We don't have to shoot them, Emmett," Kragen protested. "You know that makes me sick to my stomach. You always want to make things violent."

"Fine. I'll shoot you. Kragen here is going to close his eyes so he don't get sick to his stomach."

Somehow Billijean the Gobi fish and McGuffey the pistol shrimp had disappeared. That left the two women with their guns, the two men with **their** guns, and Christopher and Elsa with no guns in the middle.

"Maybe the two ladies should get into a shoot-out with the two gentlemen. Winner takes all. We'll just be over here watching," Christopher tried to sidle toward the train and the flattened body of Eric as he eased Elsa around the two men.

Emmett pointed one of his pistols at Christopher. "Do we look stupid to you?"

"Well, yes," Christopher admitted, then paused. "Oh. Sorry. Rhetorical question?"

Emmett just growled at him. "I'm written this way! It's not my fault."

"You could try to be different from how you're written, Emmett. Sometimes the stupid gets annoying." Kragen was watching Fonta put her gun back together again. "You ladies ever thought about going into train robberies?"

Empressa shook her head. "I don't want to get involved in train derailment That'll get you in trouble with The Conductor."

Kragen made a frantic shushing noise at her. "Don't say that name! We've managed to stay ahead of him all this time. Reckon we can stay ahead a bit longer. So, how's about it? Two of you. Two of us."

Fonta barely looked up from her gun. "I don't want the stupid one."

"Well, I don't want the stupid one," Empressa snorted.

Christopher and Elsa eased backwards toward the edge of the clearing.

"Hello," Emmett grumbled. "Right here. Listening. Look, if I could, I'd be a space cowboy. Those guys are always smart and resourceful. Everyone likes them except television execs. But I can't. I'm written just a bit on the dim side. But I can shoot a gun and I'm strong. See? Muscles." He flexed.

"What kind of gun?" Fonta finally gave him a look, although her hungry gaze seemed more for the pistols than the man holding them.

Before Emmett could answer, a new hole opened in space-time-space and the train was sucked into it. Eric's body disappeared entirely. Then a whistle blew three short blasts.

Kragen went white and his dog ears lay back flat on his head. "The Conductor. We can't be here. We gotta go. We can't be here. We gotta…". He was still trying to run away as the hole sucked him up after the train.

Emmett managed to grab a hold of Fonta who grabbed onto Empressa. The three of them rose slowly, like a kite with a long tail, gradually being sucked toward the hole in the universe.

"Run!" Elsa shouted. "We have to run!"

"But Eric. And Shiv. And we can't just…"

Elsa just grabbed Christopher's hand and started running. His only options were run with her or lose his hand. He chose to run, although he couldn't help but look backwards and watch Emmett,

Fonta, and Empressa get sucked into the hole. Then he felt it tugging at him and started to run in earnest.

"Who is this Conductor everyone is so afraid of?"

Elsa didn't seem to have any trouble running and talking at the same time. "Don't say the name," she said automatically. "He's an urban myth, a legend. No one has ever been able to say that they've seen him, but plenty of people have seen others disappear and never come back. I guess the ones who disappeared may have seen him."

"But what does he do?" Christopher wasn't nearly as good at talking and running at the same time, especially when a rip in space-time-space was trying to suck him into oblivion.

"He fixes derailed trains. Trains of thought, mostly, but some people think he works on regular trains, too. He keeps plot lines flowing around here." She pulled him behind a large tree and started unfastening his belt. "He gives characters hope that they might end up in a real plot someday."

Christopher tried to rescue his belt. "Hey, I know I wrote you to fall in love with me, but do you really think this is the time or place for you to do that?"

Elsa didn't even bother to snort. "Men. I'm trying to strap us to the tree. I hope things will go back to normal soon, but I don't think we're going to outrun anything. We just need to stay put."

Christopher quickly unfastened his belt and handed it to her. "Why didn't you say so?" He frowned. "I don't think one belt is going to do it. Or one tree. It picked up a train."

Eric appeared next to them. He looked exactly the same, except for being a touch thinner. "I have a belt. We're farther from the hole here. It might work."

Elsa put her hand out without seeming surprised. "That was fast."

"I have a respawn rule written into my character." Eric handed her the belt. "I can't stay dead for very long or I can't be killed off again." He sighed. "What I wouldn't give to be a simple vampire or zombie. They get to die once or twice and **stay** dead."

Elsa looped the two belts together, then managed to fasten them around the three of them. Christopher found it a bit snug, but wouldn't have minded if Elsa hadn't been in the middle. Eric was giving her a look that Christopher didn't at all like.

The sucking sensation grew stronger, lifting Elsa off her feet. Christopher and Eric grabbed her hands at the same time; Christopher took a second to glare at Eric before he leaned in toward Elsa. "Are you okay?"

Elsa nodded, but didn't bother to speak. She just held on tighter as the tree itself shifted.

Then the wind stopped and she fell to the ground, held up only by Eric and Christopher's grasp of her hands. The space-time-space hole had vanished. Everything was quiet.

Eric looked around, as if he'd lost something.

"What's wrong?" Elsa asked as she brushed herself off.

"I'm not dead. That was perfect fodder for dying and I'm alive. That feels wrong, somehow."

"I'd take it and be happy with it," Christopher tried to sound positive. "So, that was different. Now what?" He looked at Elsa, who grimaced.

"Why me?" She shook her head. "Come on."

Christopher was working on relooping his belt through his pants. "Where are we going?"

"We're following the road. Beyond that, I have no clue."

Eric retrieved his own belt and followed after them, forgotten again. "At least this isn't supposed to be a mystery novel.

PHOENIX FLAMBE

They walked for a very long time. The road seemed to be exactly the same: a long, straight path, just wide enough for two of them to walk abreast.[97] Elsa and Christopher walked side-by-side while Eric trailed after, just far enough behind that he was the only one killed when an elephant wearing a super hero one-piece ran through and trampled him to death. That was followed by a distant DOH!THUD! The elephant ran off and Christopher and Elsa stood staring at the hoof impressions where Eric had stood.

"What do we do?" Christopher said finally.

Elsa wrinkled her nose at Christopher. "Why do you keep asking me? Why don't you come up with any ideas yourself?"

Christopher shuffled under her stare, looking down at his feet. "Well, to be honest, I'm not a very good writer. I mean, I have ideas sometimes and I love creating characters, but I have a hard time coming up with a plot. I usually ask for help on forums when I get stuck. There aren't any forums here. Just you."

Elsa was still staring at him. "Are you getting any better?"

"At writing?" Christopher nodded. "Oh, yes. I'm definitely better than I was. I can make an entire sentence or two before I get stuck."

"Then you just need practice," Elsa decided. "So you tell me: what should we do?"

Christopher felt the slow beginnings of panic[98] squeezing his chest. "Me? But… I don't know. I don't even know what the options are. What would you do?"

Elsa sighed. "No way. You're not getting out of this. Think of it as a writing prompt. Eric just disappeared. In three sentences, tell me what happens next."

Christopher looked at Elsa just standing there, waiting, her pretty mouth set in a patient line, and he took a deep breath. "We

---

[97] It's better to walk a-hip, but it doesn't sound as cool.

[98] The fast beginnings of panic manifests as a heart attack. Much better to get a slow start in this case.

sit down and talk for a little while, waiting. A little bit of time passes while Eric does whatever he does to get his life back. Then Eric appears here." He blinked. "I did it. I thought of something."

"Yes, you did." Elsa sat, drawing him down with her, and patted his knee. "Maybe you just need practice, Christopher. Have you considered writing short stories?"

"Sure, but short stories are boring and it's National **Novel** Writing Month, not National Write What You Want Month.[99] Plus, NaWrYoWaMo sounds like a bad joke insult.[100]"

Elsa looked down at her hand on his knee, then reached over to hold his hand. "Just seems like it would be easier to start with something small for practice, then move on to something big when you get better at it."

Christopher opened his mouth, but Eric was suddenly sitting on their linked hands. "Oh, hey, guys. Did you miss me?"

Elsa let go of Christopher's hand and Eric dropped to the ground. "We waited for you," she said noncommittally.

"That's something," Eric sounded pleased. "Oh, and I brought the shrimp back with me." He pulled Shiv out of his pocket. "I couldn't leave the little guy there. The chocolate Brownies were teasing him about his booties."

"Evil creatures," Shiv muttered. "Put me down. I can walk."

"You don't have a treadmill anymore."

Shiv bit Eric's finger and Eric dropped him. "I don't need a treadmill!"

"Aren't chocolate brownies food?" Christopher tried to pick Shiv up and got his finger snapped at.

"Not chocolate brownies. Chocolate Brownies. Little sprites. They have a weird sense of humor.[101]"

---

[99] There are eleven National Write What You Want months and only one National Novel Writing month.

[100] In the not-so-secret Society of Bad Insults, NaWrYoWaMo is the punch line to a bad Yo Mama joke.

[101] Orange Brownies have no sense of humor at all, but they're much less likely to tie your knickers in a knot.

"So what do we..." Christopher started, then cut short when he saw Elsa frowning at him. "Alright. Eric is here now. We should go back to walking?"

"I don't think so, my pretties." A woman stood in the middle of the road, blocking their way. She was beautiful and terrible at the same time, with black hair pulled into an elaborate hairstyle around an even more elaborate crown. Pale skin accented her jade green eyes and dark red lips. A gorgeous green velvet dress was fitted to her form, stopping just shy of jeweled kid boots that added another four inches to her height. She held a scepter in one hand and a sword in the other and didn't look like she'd been in a good mood for at least a decade.

Christopher had had it. "I did it. I thought of what to do next and you're going to tell me no?" He picked up a branch from the side of the road. "I'm tired of you people and your silly drama and your grand entrances and exits and just all the things! All of them!" Without a breath he strode forward and smacked the sword out of the woman's hand. "I just want to go home! I want to write a novel in thirty days! Why won't anyone let me go home?" By the end of his rant, the woman was in a bloody heap on the ground and the branch was broken in two.

"Awkward," Eric spoke into the silence. "I think someone has anger issues."

"Very awkward," agreed Shiv. "She was pretty, for an evil queen."

"She was," Eric agreed in turn. "A little less pretty now. But the crown still looks nice."

Christopher just stood there breathing heavily, holding his half of the branch in one hand. Then he threw the remains of the branch on the crumpled body, turned, and stalked away. Elsa ran after him.

"Very nice flounce,[102]" Shiv noted.

---

[102] Flouncing is an artform in some cultures. There is a remote tribe in the South Pacific where there is a yearly competition for the best solo, couple, and group tantrums.

"I liked the pirouette," Eric added. "I'd give it at least an 8.5."

"His branch is smoking," Shiv noted.

It wasn't so much Christopher's branch that was smoking as it was the body it had landed on. Tiny flames started licking at the velvet fabric, then grew higher, devouring the body greedily. Soon there was nothing left but a pile of ash and the undamaged crown.

"More awkward," Eric decided.

"It was, kind of, hot," Shiv offered.

"Maybe, but any hope of a relationship with that woman just went up in smoke."

Then the ashes stirred and a very ugly bird appeared. It pecked at the ashes until the crown came free, then scooped the crown onto its head with a squawk. Then it turned and noticed Eric and Shiv. "What are you staring at?" The voice was that of a very angry woman.

"Not a thing," Shiv said.

"What he said," Eric said.

"You can't say that. I said that," Shiv argued.

"Oh, shut up," the queen-bird hissed. "I was getting tired of having to dress like a woman anyway. This form is better." Brilliant plumage in greens, blues and reds was starting to sprout from her skin. "At least the crown didn't burn."

"So you're not mad?" Eric asked.

"Because we didn't do it," Shiv offered.

"No, he did," Eric waved at Christopher, who had returned when the bird appeared and was staring at the interchange with his mouth half-open.

"No, I didn... well, I did, but I didn't mean to burn you up. Or kill you. I was just angry and you were making it worse."

The bird spread her wings, now beautifully plumed. "I make everyone angry. You're not the first person to want to kill me and you won't be the last. I was just caught by surprise. You didn't look like you had it in you." She shook out her damp feathers to dry, looking at Shiv and Eric. "I like the booties," she told Shiv archly.

Shiv turned a brighter shade of pink. "You do? I like your crown, your Majesty."

"Ellie," the queen corrected him. "But only for you."

The two of them got lost in each others' eyes and eye-stalks, Ellie giving Shiv a smouldering look that singed Eric's eyebrows and made him step to one side.

Shiv wasn't so lucky.

As Ellie and Shiv burnt to ashes, Eric looked around incredulously. "That's twice I haven't died. I wonder if I'm broken?" He whistled happily to himself, "Should we put another shrimp on the barbie?[103]"

The other two said nothing. Instead, Christopher took Elsa's hand, walked her carefully around the still-smoking pile of ash, and continued down the road.

After a moment, Eric used his belt to retrieve the hot crown from the ashes. "No reason to leave this behind. I should buy another belt. Useful item.[104]" Then he followed after them, still whistling merrily.

---

[103] Australian natives eat prawns, not shrimp, but it doesn't have quite the same ring.

[104] There is an erroneous belief that you should never go anywhere without a towel, but it should be "never go anywhere without a towel on your belt".

ACYROLOGIA

Again they walked for a very long time before Christopher called for a break. "How do you ever get anywhere here? It seems like we keep walking down the same stretch of road, past the same clump of two trees, then down a hill, past three trees, then back up a hill. It's all the same.[105]"

Elsa shrugged. "We don't really get anywhere. We walk until a writer starts the action again."

"Me?" Christopher looked around like someone might show up to be the token writer. "Oh, fine." He stopped walking. "We're there."

Out of nowhere, a fortress appeared before them. It had high, white walls, impossibly smooth, and only one gated entrance. That was guarded by a single white night.

"Hold their. Ewe cannot enter without the password."

Elsa looked at Christopher. "Does sumthing seem funny hear?"

Eric joined them. "It seams a little off, but Eye can't figure out why."

"Dew yew half the password or knot?" The night was growing restless.

"Um, know," Christopher admitted. "Ken wee common without it?"

The night scowled. "It wood bee highly irregular."

Elsa cringed. "Aim knot sir tan whey shooed go in their. Sum thing is knot write."

"Dew ewe wont two geaux?"

Withought worning, the night stepped a-sighed. "The queen wonts too sea yew. En-sighed, pleas."

Christopher looked from the weep on at the night's sighed two Elsa. "Cee y ewe shouldn't let me chews things?" He let her go bee four him. Eric fallowed after.

---

[105] Characters have been known to walk more than five hundred miles before their writer remembered to finish writing a walking chapter.

The night lead them too a throne room, oh penned the dour, and mow shunned them inn sighed.

As soon as they entered, something clicked back into place and they gave a collective sigh of relief.

"You didn't think I'd let that[106] continue in my throne room, did you?" Ellie was human again and sitting on the throne. "How annoying."

"Why would you do it at all?" Christopher asked. "That's…"

"Evil?" The queen laughed. "Exactly the point. Now, if you don't mind, I'd like my crown back. In exchange, I'll give you a free pass to your destination."

"If you're evil, why would you do that?" Elsa asked archly.

"Boredom, my dear. Besides," she fingered the necklace around her pale white throat, "I like being the most evil being here. If he stays, who knows what kind of evil would show up?"

Eric looked at the crown in his hands, then at Elsa and Christopher. He sighed. "Just when I get something nice." Dragging every step, he walked up to the throne and returned the crown.

"That's better." Ellie seated the crown on her head. Her elaborate hairdo immediately styled itself around the crown. "Time to die."

"But you said…"

"I'm sorry. Did you miss the part about being evil?" The queen clicked her tongue. "Honestly, I cannot understand why anyone trusts me. It's like you've never read a book before.[107]"

Christopher blushed. "I read books. Sometimes. I have to read for classes."

The queen waved one hand airily. "Not my concern. Time to die. If you could scream a bit, I do like that part."

The knight and two friends came into the throne room, each wielding very sharp-looking swords.

---

[106] "That" is also known as "acyrlogia".

[107] He who does not read history is destined to be surprised when it happens again.

Eric approached the first one. "Look, it's obviously a mistake. We returned the crown. If you'd just let us go, we'll be on our way."

In response, the knight swung his sword in a wide arc and removed Eric's head from his body. Elsa and Christopher backed away hastily.

"What should we do?" Elsa squeezed Christopher's hand as they backed into a wall.

"I don't know. I don't think well under pressure." Christopher winced. "I really don't want to scream like a baby."

The doors to the throne room flew open again and two women ran in. Both were wearing chain mail and carrying shields in one hand, swords in the other. "Ellie, we won't let you do this."

The queen sighed. "Oh, how pedestrian. Sisters, go away. I'm amusing myself. We can talk about this later."

The taller of the two women shook her head. "I would choose death over letting you harm another innocent being. I mean, cake would be pretty good, too, but if you insist on being difficult, then death it is.[108]"

"Oh, do be quiet, Debmi. Always such a dramatist." Ellie waved her hand and Debmi disappeared in a cloud of smoke.

The other woman quickly interposed herself between the queen and Christopher and Elsa. "Don't do this, Ellie. You don't have to be like this."

"You're a bore, Sarah. You always want to spoil my fun." Ellie idly threw a knife, which whistled past Sarah's head.

"He's a writer. You can't mess with a writer. You know that." Sarah dropped the sword and shield. "I put down my weapon. We can talk. You don't want to do this."

Ellie shook her head. "So very noble. So very boring. Be that way." She threw another knife, this one straight at Christopher's

---

[108] If granted the option for death or cake, cake is always the superior choice. If death is inevitable, at least try to have your cake and eat it, too.

head. Sarah threw herself in front of it, catching the knife in her un-mailed leg. "Still boring. I saw that coming."

Christopher reached for Elsa. "Are you okay?"

She nodded. "Are you?" she asked Sarah.

Sarah had her hand pressed tightly to her thigh, trying to stem the bleeding. "I was going to make a nice coq au vin for dinner. Maybe some crusty bread with sweet cream butter."

Ellie waved her hand again and Sarah disappeared in a puff of smoke. "Relax. They're both fine and I'm going to let you go, little writer. I want to see how this turns out, after all." She waved her hand again. Christopher ducked, but it only caused the doors to open. "Go follow your prophecy. They're usually a load of horse manure, but you can have fun with it."

"Just... go?" Christopher hadn't moved.

Ellie leaned back in her throne, clothing changing to tight, black leather. "Go away, little man, before I change my mind."

Elsa grabbed Christopher's hand. "Come on. I think she's bored."

Eric paused at the doorway. "I don't suppose I could have the crown back?"

Another knife thudded into the door frame inches from his head.

"About what I figured. Can't blame a guy for trying."

This time a knife left a thin line of blood across his cheek.

"Okay, you can." Eric slammed the door shut behind him.

YELLOW BRICK VIRUSES

"We lost Eric again."

It was the only thing Christopher could think to say. They'd run out of the castle so fast that it was a blur. Then they'd just walked. The road was still just a dirt path between two dusty fields, leading to nowhere. The sky was a dirty shade of blue, as if seen through the filter of the dirt they were stirring up as they walked.

"He'll show up." Elsa had been distracted since they left the castle, not offering any of her little side comments or observations. Not that there had been much to comment on, but it wasn't like her. When Christopher tried to draw her into conversation, her answers were monosyllabic and distant. He couldn't take the silence anymore.[109]

"What's wrong?"

"Nothing." Elsa didn't even look at him.

Christopher stopped walking. Then she looked up. "Elsa, about the only thing I know much about is you. Something's wrong. Let's talk about it."

"You're a guy. You don't talk about things."

"I'm a writer," Christopher shrugged. "Maybe I'll surprise you.[110]"

Elsa sighed. "What if she's right?"

Now Christopher was lost. "What if who's right?[111]"

"Ellie. The evil queen. What if the prophecy is all fake and doesn't mean anything?"

Christopher took a moment to think it over. "What if it is? Does it really matter?"

---

[109] As a general rule, if a normally talkative woman isn't talking, something is wrong. If a normally talkative man isn't talking, he's thinking. Or sleeping.

[110] Writers, even male writers, are far more likely to talk about things. They might be able to use it in a future book.

[111] Men's brains tend to be linear and compartmentalised. Because of this, they tend to only run two trains of thought. Women's brains tend to be random and divergent. Because of this, they will suddenly appear to change topic, when really they were thinking about eleven topics at once and just switched mental tabs. This makes cross-gender communication challenging.

Elsa was indignant. "Of course it matters! The prophecy is guiding us!"

"Is it?" Christopher balanced against a lone, stunted tree and worked a rock out of his shoe. "We can't remember most of it. The only thing we did differently because of it is have Eric come along and he keeps dying. Maybe, at some point, the prophecy will mean something, but it seems like a grocery list to me. We don't have to buy what's on it. It's just a guideline.[112]"

Elsa was staring at him, mouth open, not saying a word.

"What?"

"So that's why I love you," she said, mostly to herself. "When did you get so smart?"

Christopher shrugged uncomfortably. "Maybe it's from hanging out with you."

Elsa grinned at him. "Guest that cold be true.[113]"

"Huh?" It was his turn to stare.

"I jean I think you're tight." Elsa blushed, putting her hand to her throat.

"Are you feeling okay?"

"Go," Elsa looked like she felt anything but okay. "I thing I have an Autokorekt dire us."

Christopher looked around, then leaned in and whiskered, "Is that a mad thing?"

"Cow you have it too," Elsa wailed. "It's berry contagious![114]"

"Wee can tread it like works in the castle. Just pig snore it." Christopher didn't understand what the big deal was.

"What if you day somethink that crates something mad. Glad. Bad!" Elsa finally spit out. "Aaaahh!"

---

[112] Most people don't buy what's on their grocery list anyway, unless they're honest enough to add cookies and ice cream before they leave home.

[113] Editors and Grammar Nazis are currently suffering convulsions. Disclaimer: this book takes no responsibility for any mental or physical breakdown on the part of any person so obsessed with grammar that he or she cannot deal with minute fluctuations in the structure of it.

[114] Autokorekt viruses mutated into existence upon the arrival of cell phones and spell checkers.

Eric appeared out of nowhere, holding his decapitated head. "That hurt," he muttered as he put it back on. "But thanks for waiting." Elsa was frantically trying to wave him away. "Oh, you left on purpose?"

"We save a bug," Christopher explained.

"Why did you want to have a hug?" It took Eric a minute to realize what he'd said. "Oh." He looked at Elsa. "Autokorekt?"

She nodded.

"Cure?" Christopher asked hope fully.

"Lime. Mime. Crime." Elsa was getting frustrated. "TIME. And not walking. Stalking. TALKING."

Eric sat down next to the two of them and they all waited silently, trying not to say anything.

"Now song?" Christopher asked finally. Music started playing from somewhere and he felt a wave of dizziness.

"Maybe an horror," Elsa said dubiously. "Not sure. It's that evil spleen's fault."

They sat in silence again until Christopher could stand it no longer. "Gut why did she so it?"

Elsa puzzled out what he meant. "I don't know shed did it," she admitted. "Could must be fad timing."

Christopher shifted, trying not to talk. "Dose it go a bay faster if we don't walk?"

"I won't go," Elsa said again. Eric seemed content to sit quietly without speaking. At least he wasn't dying.

Finally, an hour was up. "Letter?" Elsa tested. "Clap!" she grumbled.

"Maybe we should walk?" Christopher suggested. "Hey, that came out all tight." He sighed. "Almost."

They all got to their feet and started walking. "Do we have a destination?" Eric asked from behind, where he was trying to draw on his hand with a marker while walking. The picture was an incredibly accurate rendering of Ellie's crown.

Christopher looked at Elsa, who shrugged. "Not really. We're just trying to figure out the prophecy."

"If you get a prophecy, I want a prophecy. I'd like to not die. Ever would be nice, but a very long time would be okay."

At that moment, a girl with shiny shoes, a living man stuffed with straw, a cyborg, and a very large lion ran past them and disappeared up the road, singing and dancing.

"That was strange," Christopher blinked. "Were they doing disco music?"

"Maybe. At least the lion didn't try to eat me," Eric said optimistically. "Maybe my prophecy is working."

Before either of the other two could say anything, a tiny dog ran up, dispatched Eric with swift efficiency, burped, ducked his head in polite apology, then ran off to rejoin his group.

"We should keep walking," Elsa suggested nervously.

"And not tempt any lions," Christopher agreed.

Neither one said a word when Eric rejoined them a few hours later, smelling vaguely of dog breath.

MUSEUM PIECES

"I'm bored," Christopher announced. "I'm tired of walking, I'm hungry, and I'm bored."

"Sometimes you have to do things when you're bored," Elsa said patiently (for the fifth time). "If you'd learn that, you'd be a better writer."

"I'm a great writer," Christopher protested. "I just have to wait for my muse to inspire me.[115] I can't write bored."

Elsa just gave him a look and he subsided.

"What's that?" He pointed.

A man was wandering down the road in front of them, dropping things on the ground. Christopher hurried ahead to pick one up.

"*Superstitious*. It's a... word?" He turned it over in his hands. The word was elaborately decorated with four-leaf clovers, black cats, and broken mirror pieces.[116] "Why would anyone be dropping words?" He picked up another. "*Triskaidekaphobia*. So he's just dropping words? That makes no sense." Sensible or not, Christopher darted ahead of the other two to catch up with the unknown man.

Elsa started to say something, then just sighed and followed. Eric picked up a word, *necrophilia*. It was decorated with tombstones. He sighed as well and threw it over his shoulder before following. No one noticed the man staring at them from behind a tree.

Christopher followed the man all the way to a little house. The house itself was made out of nothing but words, many of them

---

[115] There was once a competition between two writers to write the best short story ever. One told the judges he'd written the story to amuse them. The judges thought he said a muse helped him write the story. Writers have been dependent on their muses ever since.

No one even knows who won the competition.

[116] It's possible to guess the meaning of words in books based on context and root words. It's possible to guess the meaning of words in the book world based on decorations and whether or not it bites you. Watch out for the ones that bite.

multisyllabic and obviously freshly minted. The man opened the delicately scrolled and detailed *aperture* and disappeared inside.

Elsa caught up to Christopher just as he was about to follow the man inside. "What are you doing?"

"I just want to see what's inside. I need to return these words." Christopher didn't take his hand off the ornamental and embellished knob.

"We have to get you out of here, Christopher. Something bad is coming."

Eric caught up to them, picked a pomegranate-lychee *pavlova* off the wall of the house, and popped it into his mouth. "Not bad," he decided, looking for another food word.

"I just want to see inside, Elsa. You're not my mother. Besides, I might be able to use one of these words." Christopher pulled the door open, brushed past her, and went inside.

Inside, the room was filled, wall-to-ceiling, with exotic words. One wall was nothing but medical terminology, ranging from diseases like *fibrodysplasia ossificans progressiva* (engraved with elaborate pictures of people made completely of bone) to medicines with elaborate names like *bismuth subsalicylate* (shown as a bottle of pink stuff). Another wall was strange animals, complete with detailed pictures. A *caecillian* (an eyeless worm) chased a *weta* (a long, spiny insect) while being chased by a *Icthyophis Kohtaoensis* (a long, amphibious creature). But Christopher walked right past the wall of adjectives and adverbs to stand before the wall of verbs.

He nearly cried as he discovered that he could use *disseminate* and *promulgate* in place of the simpler "send an email" and "publish on social media". He did cry when *ruminate* replaced "think" in his mental database and *elucidate* forever took the place of "enlighten me".[117] He was so caught up in the words that he didn't notice Elsa and Eric enter the house. He also didn't see the

---

[117] Writers get emotional over new words the way anthropologists get existed over new bones. Since both the words and the bones existed before they were discovered, such an emotional response is illogical.

man he had followed as he stealthily turned a small knob. He didn't hear the door click locked. Elsa, on the other hand, noticed immediately.

"What are you doing?" She tugged on the door. "Hey! Open this door right now!" Eric moved to help her.

Christopher finally came out of his fog, standing in front of the words *chicanery, subterfuge,* and *equivocation.* "What's going on?" He found it hard to focus.

The man moved away from the knob. He was an innocuous-looking man with a smile on his face and an easy manner. He ducked his head apologetically. "I am Adam, curator of Eternia and defender of the secrets of words. This," a door hidden behind him opened and a woman joined him, "is Brenna, my employer and a curator of an entirely different sort."

Brenna was a tall redhead with striking green-grey eyes and a full figure poured into a velvet dress that matched her eyes. She touched Christopher on the arm, then jerked back as if it stung. "Nasty, this one." She moved on to Elsa. "Better, but somewhat bland." Then she touched Eric and her eyes lit up avariciously. "Oh. This one will do nicely."

Behind her, Adam was still introducing himself. "Fabulous powers were revealed to me the day I discovered words. I held aloft a book and said…"

"Oh, can it, Adam. No one cares." Brenna was walking around Eric, hampered only slightly by the fact that he was trying to melt into the wall behind him and Elsa was still standing next to him.

"I care," Adam cringed at her words, but closed his mouth and escaped through the door she'd come in. It snicked shut, then locked behind him.

"Now, my pretty, what shall I do with you?" Brenna grabbed Eric's left ear and led him to a seat. "I don't have any cages left for living specimens, but I do hate to kill you off."

"Kill me?" Eric sighed. "Isn't anyone original anymore?"

Brenna acted as if she hadn't heard him. Her face was pretty enough, but her nose was long and, unfortunately, quite pointed.

She used it to sniff Eric. "Such a moist, tasty little tidbit. Yes, I must have you. The other two can go."

"Hurtful, but okay. Talk to you some other time." Christopher started edging toward the door before Elsa hissed at him.

"We need him!"

He hissed back, "If she kills him, he'll be free. Let's go before she changes her mind."

There was, apparently, nothing wrong with Brenna's ears. "Free? Oh, no. He can't go free. He's going to be part of my… collection." She rubbed her hands together. "I'll just keep him alive and kill one of the others." She jumped as *atrocious* hit her in the cheek. "Stop that! You put those back!"

Elsa took another word from the nearest wall. "I will not. Eric is going with us. I'll just keep throwing things at you until you let him go."

"Really," Eric protested from behind her, "if she's not going to kill me, I don't mind staying."

Elsa gave him a dirty look.

"Or I could go," Eric equivocated. "Yes, probably should go. Sorry. It was nice meeting you…"

"No, you're not going!" Brenna screeched. She grabbed Eric by the arm, her fingers elongating into claws.

"Pinching," Eric noted in a pained voice. "Little painful… ow. Hurting here."

Brenna wasn't paying any attention to him. Her focus was on Elsa. "So there's more to you than you appear," she mused. "Maybe I should keep you as well."

"Excuse me!" Christopher was finally affronted. "I'm here, too."

"Way to stick up for me, Lothario," Elsa rolled her eyes, then caught them before they rolled out of reach. "That's all you have to say?"

Christopher shrugged. "She wants everyone but me. I'm a little hurt."

"Maybe you could be hurt **after** we escape? Just a thought."

Eric was ignoring the entire exchange in favor of watching his arm slowly turn green. "That can't be healthy," he observed thoughtfully, face still scrunched up in pain.

Brenna ignored him back and didn't let go. "You're not right," she told Christopher. "You make my skin crawl."

Christopher's face fell. "Still hurtful."

"Could you pout any more childishly?" Elsa asked him. "You hurt her. That means you can help us escape, genius."

Christopher brightened. "It does, doesn't it?" He approached Brenna. "Let me show you what hurting feels like."

Brenna tried to back away, but the wall was behind her, Eric was caught in her clawed hand next to her, and there was nowhere to go. "Don't touch me," she squealed. "Don't touch me!"

Eric's entire arm was green now. "Guys, I think this might be bad. Guys?"

Elsa tried to pull Eric away from Brenna, but the green was spreading faster. She pulled back before it could touch her. "You don't look too good."

"I don't feel too good," Eric agreed. "If this is a new way to die, I'll go back to simple poison."

Christopher touched Brenna and she screamed. Then she dissolved. It started, slowly, with her long nose folding in on itself, then sped down her face until she was a sagging mask. The rest of her body followed suit until she was just a large puddle. Then she evaporated.

Unfortunately, Eric turned green at about the same rate as Brenna dissolved. By the time Brenna evaporated, Eric was an oversized book with green binding.

"Didn't see that coming," Christopher mused. "Do you think he'll be a bestseller? What happens if someone tries to read him?"

Elsa gingerly touched Eric. He didn't move. "He's not dead; I can still feel a heartbeat."

"That's good, right? I mean, he wanted to stop dying."

"But if he doesn't die, then he's stuck like this. He'll be a book forever."

Christopher looked at Elsa. Then he looked at Eric. Then, slowly, he looked back at Elsa again. "We could burn him up."

"Are you crazy?"

"You wanted me to come up with ideas! This is my idea. If we burn him, he dies and comes back as Eric. Tearing pages out would just be destructive. Otherwise, we leave him like this and he's a book forever." Christopher's shoulders sagged. "I don't know what else to do, Elsa. I know he said he didn't want to die anymore, but I don't think he wanted to live as a book, either. Who would?"

"A tree?" In spite of her tart answer, Elsa didn't sound certain. "I don't know. There has to be something else."

Christopher sat down on the floor. He was tired and no one seemed to think about eating unless they were written to eat all the time.[118] "I'm open to ideas if you have them. This is the best I could do."

Elsa paced in front of Eric for a long time, then sighed. "Alright, let's do it"

Christopher shook himself awake. "Do it?"

"Let's burn him up. If he doesn't come back, I'm blaming you."

"That sounds about right for my life," Christopher sighed. "Do you have matches?"

Elsa looked at him steadily.

"What? It's a question."

"You created me in detail, Christopher. Did you create any matches in my pockets?"

"No," Christopher scowled. "Maybe you picked some up."

"Did you?"

Christopher's scowl just deepened in reply.

---

[118] Most characters in development either spend most of their stories eating or none of it. Characters don't become well-rounded until they have a book.

"Thought not." Elsa started looking through the words, tossing them randomly over shoulder after she read them. "*Humectation.* No. *Saturated.* Uh-uh. *Drizzle.*" She sighed. "Wrong section." She slid down the row a bit. "*Conflagration.* Oh, yes, this will do nicely." She slid the word out of its space. "You may want to get ready to run."

"Um, door's locked," Christopher reminded her.

"Find a word to open it, then."

Christopher randomly picked up a word. "*Unimpede.* I have no idea what that means." He started to toss it aside.

"No, no. Keep it! That will work." Elsa carefully set *conflagration* next to Eric. "I hope this works."

The door opened behind them.

BUYING THE ZOO

A large dragon waddled in. She was black overlaid with rain slick colors: shimmers of purple, green, blue and yellow that ran the length of her glistening leather skin. She was also obviously pregnant, with the discernible shapes of at least three baby dragons in her bulging belly.

"Christopher! While I'm honoured to be reincarnated as a dragon, really, a pregnant female? Do I look like a good choice to be a pregnant female?" The dragon settled her bulky form down right in front of the doorway.

"Do I know you?" Christopher peered at the unfamiliar form, although he felt a tingling twinge of familiarity at the word "reincarnated".

The dragon stomped one forefoot, making the house shake and words fall off the shelves. "I AM SHIV! Or I was, before this last reincarnation. Now I'm Shivani. Really, the rug rats battling inside my belly are the final insult. I'm afraid you are toast. Writer flambe. BE STILL, YOU LITTLE MONSTERS!" she bellowed as her stomach distended and quivered in nausea-inducing waves.

Christopher retreated. "I'd really rather not burn to death."

"I DIDN'T WANT TO BURN EITHER," Shivani bellowed. "SEE WHERE THAT GOT ME?"

Christopher winced and rubbed at his earlobes. "Caps lock,[119] guy. Lady. Whatever. Do you have to yell so much?"

Shivani poked at one of the bulges in her belly with her snout. "You try being pregnant. I don't have the disposition for this. If it weren't my own belly, I'd just burn them out." Her eyes glowed orangish-red. "I'll have to content myself with burning you out."

"You really don't want to do that." It was a suggestion born of desperation, but Christopher had to try.

"Yes, I think I really do," Shivani decided. "DIE, WRITER!"

---

[119]   Only a writer would call this caps lock instead of yelling. Most people just call it rude.

She shot a stream of flame at Christopher. The flame caught the word *conflagration* first, setting a merry blaze. It devoured *humectation, saturation,* and *drizzle* without a pause. Then Eric started to burn.

"Still need practice," Shivani growled. "This is harder than it looks. DON'T LAUGH AT ME!"

Christopher wasn't laughing, although Elsa was making a convoluted combination of motions from thumbs-up to frantic waves for him to get himself away from the fire. Then she was shoved aside from behind.

"There you are." A slender woman with a long pike in one hand and thick chains wound about her body[120] strode into the room, ignoring the raging fire. "I've been tracking you quite a distance. A dragon with babies. Perfect. You'll make a great addition to my zoo."

"ZOO?" Shivani didn't sound at all flattered. "I DON'T BELONG IN A ZOO!"

The woman popped earplugs into her ears. She was barely clothed under the chains.[121] "Bellowing doesn't work on me, but good of you to try." She reached down to offer a hand up to Elsa. "You might want to go on and get out of here. This could get a little warm. I'm Kit, by the way. My zoo is just up the road apace if you want to stop by and see the specimens. I only charge if none of the animals eat you. Great deal."

Christopher had edged away from the Eric-inferno and was now standing next to Elsa. "We might have to pass, quest and all, but good luck. What about the babies?"

"THE BABIES?" Shivani screeched. "WHAT ABOUT ME?"

Kit's eyes reflected the raging flame. "Oh, the babies are good eating. Besides, a dragon is far easier to control when recovering from forced birth." She twirled the pike. "Time to make me rich."

---

120 This would be implausibly heavy and clumsy, marking her as a character from a fantasy world or barbarian romance novel.

121 Only in fantasy worlds do the warriors wear less clothing than the average population. This is otherwise known as The Barbarian Lingerie Law.

Suddenly, a huge woman ran into the room. She was at least three hundred pounds poured into a bunny costume with less than flattering effect and had earrings dangling from her oversized, pink ears. "Party? Party! Hey, there, I'm Cherylee," she reached out to shake Elsa's hand, then changed her mind and patted her on the head with a paw the size of a dinner plate. She swatted Christopher on the backside as she hopped past with far more agility than one would expect, making him jump.

Kit looked from Shivani to Cherylee, her pike remaining trained on the dragon. "What are you doing here? This is my dragon."

"I AM NO ONE'S DRAGON," Shivani bellowed. No one paid much attention to her bellow at this point, although the babies in her belly moved more when she yelled.

"Oh, I don't want the dragon. Not when there's already a perfect fire going." Cherylee ran right past the pike-wielding zoo collector, then the dragon, embracing the pillar of fire that was Eric. "You're, like, hot,[122]" she crooned. "Great balls of fire, baby."

Christopher edged halfway out the door. "She's crazy. They're all crazy. We should go."

Elsa stopped him with a hand on his arm. "But Shivani. Okay, not really a friend, but can you just leave her here like this?"

Christopher hesitated. "She wants to burn me to a crisp. I might be able to get over the guilt, but I'm pretty sure I don't get over being turned into writer flambe."

There was now no distinguishing between Eric and Cheralee as they burned merrily together. Kit shrugged and turned her attention back to Shivani. "So, how should we get those babies out of your belly? The hard way or the easy way?"

"I'm inclined toward the easy way," Shivani said, waddling sideways toward the door. "Teleportation if possible. If not, lots of drugs. All the drugs. Overwhelming doses of pharma."

---

[122] The misuse of the word "like" in a non-metaphorical situation is a Class V offense and is punishable by being forced to listen to eighty hours of electronic music while wearing leg warmers.

Kit didn't seem to move, but she was suddenly standing between Shivani and the door. "I don't believe in letting foreign substances taint my specimens, sorry. But I could teleport the babies out of you one at a time." She shoved the butt end of the pike into the floor, sharp end toward Shivani. "It might hurt. Actually, it will hurt. Might as well be honest about it."

The fire was now large enough to singe the walls near Shivani. Her black skin was glowing orange and red. "What are my other options?"

Kit smiled in a wide, eager show of teeth. "I could cut them out of you. Either way, it's going to hurt."

Shivani looked directly at Christopher. "Kill me," she said evenly.

Christopher blinked and looked behind him for someone else. "Me? Why me? You already hate me."

Shivani had moved as far back from Kit as possible. "Because I reincarnate, you idiot, and I'd rather not be a specimen in a zoo. KILL ME."

Christopher felt the bellow envelope him. He grabbed the nearest word behind him and threw it at Shivani, who read it as it hit her.

"*Defenestration*. What the…"

The building exploded.

PUNKS AND STEAM

When Christopher regained consciousness, he was lying sprawled on his back in an ashy field next to the road. The house was nothing more than a mound of smoking embers. Elsa was next to him, still unconscious. Kit, Eric, and Cherylee were nowhere to be seen.

Shivani— possibly Shiv— was now a tiny gray mouse. "Not a word," it squeaked at him. "NOT ONE WORD." The yelling wasn't very effective at mouse volume.[123]

Christopher sat up, brushed ash out of his hair, and gently shook Elsa. "I didn't say anything. What happened to the others?"

Shivani cleaned herself with her paws. "I didn't fit through the window, so the window exploded and I died. Instant reincarnation. Two burnt up. The babies flew off when I changed— instant birth, I suppose. Last I saw, the evil zoo woman was chasing them."

"And him?" Christopher pointed to a smoking man who was just standing at the edge of the clearing, staring at them intently.

Shivani flicked her tail. "He's just been standing there, staring. He doesn't seem to be burning, just smoking. I don't know why."

As if triggered by them talking about him, the man turned and disappeared. An elephant on a tricycle chased after him, followed by a distant DOH!THUD.

"Back to normal now, I guess," Christopher said wearily. Elsa stirred beside him and he helped her sit up. "How are you feeling?"

Elsa wiped blood from her cheek. "Like a dragon exploded," she admitted. Her eyes lit on the mouse. "Shiv?"

"Still Shivani," the mouse twitched.

Elsa struggled to her feet. "I guess it's time to walk."

Christopher jumped up and put his arm around her waist. "Are you up to it?"

---

[123] Dragon volume ranges from loud to deafening. Mouse volume ranges from too quiet for human ears to loud enough to annoy a cat.

That tugged a hint of a smile from Elsa. "**Now** you find chivalry. Cute. I'll manage."

"What about me?" Shivani asked from the ground. "You're not leaving me behind, are you?"

Elsa looked at Christopher, who shrugged. "The last time someone offered you a ride, you threatened to bite. You can ride in a pocket or on a shoulder," he said finally. "Amends for whatever wrong you think I've done to you."

Shivani ran up his pant leg and over his chest to his shoulder. "Forgiven," she said as she perched near his ear. "Just don't do it again."

Christopher shook his leg and rubbed his chest. "Don't do that again either," he frowned. "Tiny mouse feet tickle and that was a little close to more intimacy than I'm really looking for from a mouse."

Shivani just flicked her tail at him and feigned interest in the road ahead.

They started walking again, Elsa slowly recovering enough strength to pull away and walk alone. Christopher found himself wishing she hadn't, but didn't say anything. Once again it was an endless road under a pale blue sky with empty green fields to either side.

"What is that?" Shivani twitched her tail toward the air and Christopher and Elsa stopped to look up.

A huge balloon was floating several hundred feet in the air toward them. It was made of brightly colored patches in a seemingly random pattern and was almost festive, except for the guns bristling all around the outside edge of the basket.[124]

"That looks like another delay," Christopher sighed. Then he was pulled to the ground from behind.

"Are you right daft, man? Stay down. It's harder for them to get a proper fix that way. Patrick," he added by way of introduction.

---

[124] In some novels, it wouldn't be considered at all festive without a few guns. Your point of view may vary.

Patrick and another man were lying prone behind them. Both wore brown leather greatcoats, brown bowler hats, and sturdy brown boots. Patrick had a thick black beard and a long-barreled gun. The other had long brown hair pulled into a neat queue and a shorter gun with lots of attachments. "Sorry for the pull. I'm Jeffrey," he nodded to Elsa. "Faster than explaining."

"Elsa," Christopher motioned, "Christopher. Oh, and Shivani." In response, the mouse bit him on the ear.

"See?" Christopher rubbed away the small spot of blood. "I *knew* you'd bite me."

"Might get another pet. That one's mean," Patrick observed.

"Pet?" Shivani squeaked indignantly.

Elsa was about to respond when two women walked up the road. One was a tall blonde, slender and bespeckled. The other was shorter, with dark hair and skin. Both wore a mound of petticoats under frilly dresses and carried parasols. They were talking quietly, heads together, as if completely oblivious to the five on the ground.

When they got closer, Patrick and Jeffrey rose to pull them to the ground as well. Then the parasols were replaced with long-barreled pistols.

"I really shouldn't do that if I were you," the smaller one suggested. "Britnee gets a bit quick on the trigger when she's nervous." Her dress was a pale powder blue that contrasted sharply with her dark complexion.

"I do not, Jane," the blonde said with a frown. "I just like the smell of black powder." Her dress was a darker green and more elaborately embroidered. "Besides, this one is fair handsome, in a rough way. I'd hate to shoot him."

Jane sniffed at her. "I saw him first."

"Did not," Britnee argued. "I saw him first."

"There are two of them," Elsa offered helpfully. "Oh, and a balloon or dirigible or whatever with lots of guns flying our way."

Both women turned to look. "Oh, how nice. I haven't seen one of those in some time. I do wish I'd brought my cannon," Jane said with a hint of a sigh. "You didn't bring a cannon, did you, Brit?"

Britnee shook her head. "Just the pistol." She settled her skirts around her as she lay flat on the ground next to Patrick. "Do you have a cannon, sir?[125]"

Jane stretched out on his other side, pointing her pistol at the balloon. "I bet he has quite a cannon,[126]" she said.

"Not on me, ladies," Patrick patted his gun. "Only this.[127]"

"Do they even know you're here?" Christopher asked Jeffrey, who shrugged and smiled.

"He's written as the cad no one can figure out who somehow gets all the women. I'm written as the sidekick who saves the day but goes home alone each night with the readers rooting for me. I'd rather be me, to be honest."

The balloon was now directly overhead, but seemed unable to stay still long enough for the gunners to aim at the stationary figures on the ground. There was a stray burst of gunfire, but the bullets all went far left.

Patrick removed a metal contraption from the large pockets of his greatcoat and opened it, revealing a tripod for his gun. He sped through setting it up, haphazardly slapping together each piece, then attached the base of his gun to the top.

"I love a man who's prepared," Britnee cooed.

Jane just edged closer on Patrick's other side without a word.

Shivani muttered near Christopher's ear, "I hate simpering women."

Christopher jumped, nearly knocking Shivani off her perch. "Don't *do* that! I forgot you were there. Besides, aren't you a simpering woman now?"

---

[125] In some books, this is a standard greeting; in others, it borders on innuendo. In this instance, it may be both.

[126] Still borderline innuendo.

[127] Normal male missing borderline innuendo.

That earned him another nip to his ear. "You should be paying more attention. I'm a female mouse, not a woman. I don't simper. There isn't enough bad karma in all the world to turn me into a simpering woman."

Jeffrey was quietly setting up a device with a multitude of dials and knobs, all shiny and metal. Elsa watched with interest. "What is that?"

"I haven't come up with a name yet," he said in his careful way, attention still on the device. "Ground to air defense." At her blank look, he smiled. "It lobs things into the air that explode when they hit something. In this instance, when they hit the balloon."

"Not if I get them first," Patrick called over, setting his gun's sights. "May the better man win," he saluted Jeffrey.

Jeffrey saluted back. "After you," he said with a sweep of his arm.

Patrick hunkered down behind his gun, the two women moving back just enough to give him room to work. There was a collective holding of breath as Patrick aimed, then a mutual expulsion as he fired.

For a long, hopeful moment, nothing happened. Then one of the guns on the balloon exploded in a rain of shrapnel and chorus of screams.

Patrick looked pleased with himself. "Your turn," he motioned to Jeffrey as the two women jostled to congratulate him first.

Jeffrey turned a knob, wound a dial, and carefully aimed his device. Then he waited.

And waited.

Britnee peeked over. "Is it broken?"

"No," Jeffrey said calmly. "Just not ready yet."

A full minute more passed with nothing happening, then everything happened at once.[128]

---

[128] The National Order of the Natural Order of Things requires a notice here that it is impossible for everything to happen at once in real life, let alone in a book. The proper sequence of events is listed, although most may not notice the .0012 millisecond pause between events.

The balloon exploded in a blossom of fire that compressed inward before spreading outward, showering sparks on the ground.

Jeffrey's device exploded in a cacophony of bells, whistles, gears and steam.

Shivani darted off Christopher's shoulder at exactly the wrong time to have a flying gear crush her.

Christopher threw himself over Elsa and tried to compact them both into a tight ball.

Patrick spread his leather greatcoat out and the woman dove beneath it. The area around them immediately became blurred as they were temporarily moved to a book with parental guidance warnings on the front.[129]

Then things stopped happening all at once as the balloon crashed to the ground in a disappointing hiss of smoke.

Jeffrey pulled an extinguisher from his greatcoat and put out the blaze his machine had become. "That wasn't supposed to happen," he mused. "Back to the drawing board."

Christopher gingerly let Elsa get up. "Are you alright?"

She didn't move. "You did something brave."

"Did I hurt you or are you in shock? You sound shocked. You don't need to sound shocked."

Elsa kissed him, effectively shutting him up.

Jeffrey looked over, smiled to himself, and finished cleaning up. Then he disappeared with the pieces of his machine.

It wasn't the most perfect kiss. Both participants were badly in need of a toothbrush and some mouthwash and their noses bumped in awkward places. It wasn't the most passionate kiss. They had to sidestep a flying metal seat somewhere in the middle and nearly stepped on the fallen body of Shivani. It wasn't even

---

[129] Temporal displacement within books may occur at any point during writing, editing, or review. Sometimes it occurs decades after the book is published, when it is randomly put on a banned book list and eagerly sought by millions of readers who might otherwise have skipped it entirely.

the most romantic kiss, since Christopher had random male thoughts that earned him a slap near the end of it.

It didn't matter. It was a kiss and they both meant it. Writer and character, they seized the moment[130] and fell completely in love.

An earthquake shook the ground. They clung together more tightly. Lightning zig-zagged across the sky as it blackened with thick, rolling clouds, then opened in pouring rain. Still they kissed (after the slap), ignoring soppy wet clothing and mud squishing into their shoes. They paid no attention to the few survivors of the balloon, limping out and collapsing until the rain put out their fires.

The sky darkened further and a long, jagged line formed, spreading from one end of the horizon to the other. The injured characters whimpered in terror and dragged themselves off the sodden field. Patrick, Jane, and Britnee peeked out from beneath the greatcoat, then disappeared permanently, greatcoat and all.

Still they kissed.

"I love you," Elsa breathed at last.

Christopher touched her face. "You have to love me," he said wistfully. "I wish you didn't."

"Fine. I like you **and** I love you," Elsa kissed his chin, although she'd been aiming for his nose. "I don't have to like you."

Christopher looked hopeful. "You like me?"

"I do," she nodded. "I've tried not to, but I do."

They stood like that, rain buffeting around them, just savouring the moment. "Are you allowed to like me?" Christopher asked.

"Christopher!"

He shrugged. "Seems like we're not allowed to do a lot of things. Are you allowed to like me?"

"I don't know," Elsa admitted. "I've never liked someone before. I didn't expect to like you now." She shifted against him, nearly stepping on the dead mouse again.

---

[130] They would have had a "carpe diem" moment, but Christopher had a seafood allergy and wasn't sure he could tolerate the fish of the day.

"Poor Shivani," Christopher said. "Hope she or he returns soon. I wonder what happened to the others?"

Elsa picked up a stray bit of metal. "I think they found somewhere to go. When did it start raining?"

Christopher looked up. "When did a giant line open up in the sky?"

"Oh, that's not good." Elsa swallowed. "That's not good at all."

"Why?"

Elsa backed away from him, then grabbed his hand. "This would be a good time to run."

"Why?"

She thwapped him. "Run now. Ask later. If you ask why again, I won't like you nearly as well."

Christopher shut up and they ran.

ACRYLIC NAILS

Holy scribe, they've messed things up!

Oh, Rachel here again. I know. You missed me. Get over it; I had things to do. On the other hand, look how pretty my nails are now. Actually, on both hands. It'd be silly just to do one hand.

Back to the dunce duo. Everyone knows you can't mix worlds. It doesn't matter what the medium: if you try to bring two people together from two different worlds, stuff goes boom. Shakespeare. Broadway. Fairy tales. Action movies. You just don't do it.[131]

So, this is bad. Chances are pretty good that they just triggered massive bookageddon or some sort of -pocalypse. Pretty tacky, if you ask me. Especially over a kiss. Go kiss your own kind.

Not you! You're supposed to be sitting here reading, not kissing. Ugh. Readers.

Anyway, you're probably a little bit lost with everything that's going on, but you'll just have to play catch up on your own time. This is my time.

The one thing I will help you out with is the rules. See, writers and characters can't connect like that. Oh, the random "in love with your character" thing or writing a character to be in love with you (which is inconsiderate, really, because it means they have no choice in the matter) is one thing. Those are kind of cute in a gag-inducing way and, like character crushes, really don't affect anyone outside of the two people involved.[132]

Once a writer and a character actually connect though— kiss or more— it affects everyone around them. The writer wants to be with the character. The character wants to be with the writer. It's one big, sloppy, nasty mess.

---

[131] Actually, action movies do it all the time, since higher explosion rate equals higher box office totals.

[132] Random characters in genres ranging from romantic comedy to tragedy would disagree with Rachel's assessment. It should be noted that Mercutio and Benvolio put aside their differences long enough to file a joint lawsuit against her for Improper Assessment of Character Impact. The case is still pending.

It also creates a plot tear or hole, which makes The Conductor mad. If you haven't figured it out yet, making The Conductor mad is a Very Bad Thing. It's a Very Bad Thing on the level of dropping a rampaging bull into a stadium full of children. No, toddlers. Maybe even infants. Yeah, it's more like dropping a dozen hungry dinosaurs into a stadium full of helpless, innocent babies. Very Bad Thing.

Alright, I admit I've never seen The Conductor and this is mostly gossip, but rumor has it he doesn't like anyone to be happy unless it's required in the plot.[133] He'll do anything to save the plot, but writers don't **have** a plot. Writers are supposed to make plots, not join them. So it makes The Conductor mad. Really mad.

Anyway, I still have a few things to do before the apocageddon fun. I have a dress picked out, but I need new shoes. Maybe a purse. Then it's time to pop some popcorn, get something strong to drink, and sit back to watch the fireworks.

What do you mean, get involved? What would I do? I can tell them what I know, but I don't think it will change anything. They just need to do their little quest, not kiss, and hopefully avoid The Conductor until they get writer boy back to his own world. Simple.

If you want to get involved, you tell them, but that kind of reader-character thing only really worked in *Peter Pan*.[134] Good luck making that work here.

Tell you what: I'll save you some popcorn and pour an extra drink if you're still here. Cheers.

---

[133]   The Writer's Conspiracy Council is currently conducting a study that the recent upswing in stories involving at least one character death per book may be directly attributed to The Conductor.

[134]   Unsubstantiated rumor holds that Wendy Darling was actually a writer who fell in love with Peter Pan, with Tinkerbell being an unintended victim. Peter had so much guilt over Tink's death that he petitioned readers to save her life.

A GAME OF BRIDGES

Running doesn't do any good when you're running from the sky. Christopher decided that right about the time that his lungs exploded, escaped out his nose, and left him bent over and near-retching, trying to force blood to his aching muscles.

Elsa looked almost as tired, in spite of being a character, but she still tried to urge him on. "We need to move."

"We... can't." Christopher waited until he could talk without sounding like a bad actor. "We can't run away from it and we can't run toward it. It's everywhere, Elsa. It's the sky."

Elsa shook her head. "We're not running away." She pushed a braid out of her face, wiping sweat away from her eyes. "We're running toward the end of the prophecy. We have to get there before The Conductor shows up." She took his face in her hands, grimaced, and wiped her sweat-covered hands on his shirt, then spoke to him without touching. "We have to finish the quest and send you back."

"I don't want to go back. I want to stay here with you."

Elsa gave him a wistful smile. "I'd like that, too, but I like being alive and knowing you're alive. The Conductor will spit us both out like kindling."

Before Christopher could correct her metaphor, Eric and Shiv appeared at the same time. Eric was no longer a book, but he still had a green tinge to his skin. Shiv was human and male again, even if his ears seemed a little oversized. Both looked around, then at each other, then at themselves.

"Oh, finally," Shiv sighed in relief. "I was afraid it'd be warthog or something next."

Eric traced one of the green lines running along his left arm, but otherwise left them alone. "Thanks," he told Shiv. "Not only did you burn me to death, but I will never get rid the feel of dying with that woman wrapped around me."

"I thought you didn't want to be a book forever," Shiv protested.

"We thought so, too," Christopher offered.

115

"Not particularly, but do you know how much burning hurts? I think I still have bits of that woman burnt into my being. Woman. Burnt. Into. Me.[135]" He shuddered. "That's going to take some time and counseling to recover from." He looked around. "Why are we just standing here and what did you do to the sky?"

"Why do you think we did it?" Christopher asked defensively.

Eric didn't say a word.

"Okay, so we might have kissed. Elsa thinks The Conductor is coming."

Shiv backed away from them. "Not that I'm not grateful for being pregnancy- and dragon baby free. Not that I don't appreciate being human again. Not that you're not both very nice people, overall. But I don't think I want to be involved in anything where 'The Conductor is coming' is the key phrase."

Eric looked at the sky again. "I hear if The Conductor gets you, you die permanently. That would be different, at least. I'm still in."

Elsa blinked. "Even after the burning?"

"Eh, it did free me from the book. What's a little burning between friends?[136]" Eric shrugged. "It wasn't poison. The green stuff might have been poison, but the burning was just different."

Elsa gave him an impulsive hug. "Thank you, Eric. I'm pretty sure you're important to the prophecy. I would have hated to handcuff you and drag you with us."

"Handcuffs?" Eric opened his mouth, caught the look on Christopher's face, and snapped it shut. He returned Elsa's hug, then slunk backwards before Christopher could find out if 'looks could kill' was literal. "Yeah, me too," he said finally.

Shiv looked at the three of them. "You all suck," he announced balefully. "But I'll come, too."

---

[135]   Due to copyright issues, the editor removed all the song title puns that used to be here, but this mention should be enough to drag a few out of the recesses of memory as earworms.

[136]   This is filed under "Things You'd Never Hear at Pompeii" AND "Things to Never Say to Mrs. O'Leary".

Elsa kissed him on the cheek. "Thank you, Shiv."

"Why does he get a kiss?" Eric asked.

Christopher frowned. "Do I get a hug or kiss for coming?"

That earned him a thwap. "You already had your kiss. That's why we're running, remember?"

He sighed. "If we already triggered the end of the world, might as well kiss a few more times.[137]" He puckered up.

Eric started walking. "I wouldn't push it. Women get touchy about first kisses. When your first kiss triggers the end of the world, I'm gonna guess the touchy factor is exponential.[138]"

"End of the world?" Christopher followed after him. "No, just the end of us. The Conductor isn't happy with us. I get that. But I don't think he has anything against the whole world."

Shiv looked at Eric. "You should tell them."

"Maybe you could tell them," Eric said diffidently. "You're better at mean than I am."

"Unkind," Shiv told him. "True, but still unkind." He linked one arm through Christopher's and the other through Elsa's. "Time for a little reality, children. See the sky up there? While I'm sure your kiss was very earth-shaking, life-shattering, overwhelmingly important to the two of you… that's really not worth that sky up there. The Conductor could just open a little hole, grab you both up, and be done with it. Remember the train robbers?" He sounded like he was almost enjoying sharing the bad news. "That sky up there is reserved for Very Bad Things. End of the world things. Armageddon. The Apocalypse. Apocageddon. Armocalypse. Whatever mixture of 'oh, horror, horror, we're all going to die!' floats your boat, that's what we've got here. This is the kind that no combination of "only mostly dead," "not dead yet", and endless respawn will overcome."

Eric gave him a golf clap. "Very nicely done."

---

[137] This works about as well as "if you already have a headache, sex can't possibly make it worse".

[138] Possibly on a level with finding out that giving your virginity to a man just turned him into a heartless creature with no soul.

"Thank you," Shiv bowed. "Not too blunt? Too melodramatic? I'm a little worried about the melodrama level."

"No, not at all. Just the right touch, I'd say."

"Wait," Christopher interrupted. "You're saying that the sky up there is because the entire world is ending? So… finishing the prophecy or quest may not fix it?"

Eric looked at Shiv. Shiv looked back at Eric. "Your turn. Besides, I'm parched. I need a drink. Does anyone have something to drink?"

"What happens if you finish the quest?" Eric prompted.

Elsa sighed. "Christopher goes home, we hope." She sounded glum.

"And what happens if you go home?" Eric asked Christopher.

"I'm a sad, lonely, loser of a wannabe-writer again," Christopher's sigh sounded more pathetic than Elsa's. "If you're trying to motivate me, you're terrible at it."

Eric looked back at Elsa. "What happens if he goes home?"

Elsa stopped and thought for a long moment. "We stop the end of the world?"

"Bingo!" Eric tapped the end of her nose. "Front of the class, young lady. Gold star!" Shiv gave him a high-five.

Suddenly, Christopher stopped walking. "What time is it?"

Eric kept walking and ran into his back and Shiv and Elsa nearly got yanked off their feet. "What does that matter?"

"The prophecy. Bridge at eight. Do we know where a bridge is?"

"We don't even know where the other people are, Christopher. It's just us." Elsa looked around them. "Same long, empty road made of dirt. Same barren, empty fields to either side. Same sky, except for the huge Hole of Doom stretching across it."

He shook his head. "We'll worry about that later." At her scowl, he shrugged. "You wanted me to start thinking. This is me thinking. What time is it?"

Shiv wasn't wearing a watch, but Eric was. "Six sixteen."

"Then we have almost two hours." Christopher looked up at the sky. "Does The Conductor have to follow prophecies?"

There was a long silence.

"No one knows?" Christopher looked at each of them. "You know all these things, but not that?"

The other three shook their heads, almost in unison. "It's all urban legend. No one ever sees The Conductor and returns to talk about it. That's the whole point," Elsa explained.

Christopher started walking. "Then we'll just have to hope he follows some rules, too. If we can fix this by eight, then I think he'll leave us alone."

"And why is that?" Shiv asked. "Magical writer powers that let you know how things work even though you can't figure out how to fix them?"

Christopher grinned. "Maybe. Or maybe I just remembered that the last time we saw a hint of The Conductor, he acted very quickly. The train robbers disappeared in less than five minutes. Then the conductor disappeared. Time is passing and nothing's happening except scary clouds and ground shakes."

"He has a point," Eric conceded.

Elsa patted Christopher's cheek. "He does have them occasionally."

"Less patronizing, more congratulating," Christopher grumbled. "So, where is the bridge?"

The other three all started talking at once.

"Over the Grand River…"

"… has to be near that castle…"

"… four bridges all in the same place."

"STOP."

Everyone looked at Christopher. "Caps lock," Shiv said mildly.

"How many bridges are in this place?"

Eric mused. "Nine thousand, give or take."

"We can't be at all of them by eight," Christopher noted. "So which one is the right one?"

No one said a word.

119

"You all live here. Isn't there a bridge that is **the** bridge?"

Slowly they all shook their heads. "Different writers. Different bridges."

"Did you ever create a bridge?" Elsa asked.

"No. Just you," Christopher said glumly.

"Hey!" she smacked him. "Less glum, more 'glad you're here for the ride'."

He kissed her. "Sorry. Now you see how it feels." Clouds parted and peals of thunder played drumrolls across the sky. "Sorry again," Christopher coughed. "No kissing. Got it."

Eric squeezed between Christopher and Elsa. "I offer myself as barrier to keep you from doing stupid things."

Shiv squeezed in on her other side. "I agree."

"Probably no consequences if we kiss her," Eric suggested.

Shiv nodded. "Should be tested, just to be safe."

They leaned in from either side. Elsa leaned back from them at the last possible second and they plowed mouth-first into each other instead.

"What was that for?" Shiv protested, pulling back quickly. "Bros, yes. Mates, yes. Playmates, not."

"I am **not** kissing either of you and, if you can't behave, we'll do this without you!" Elsa snapped, stamping her foot. "Think you can behave?"

"Do we hab to?" Eric asked. His lower lip was swollen and bleeding slightly from where his teeth had gone through it. Elsa just glared at him.

Shiv wiped his mouth. "Rather unfair, but fine. I can certainly keep my hands off you. Your toenails don't even match."

"That's intentional," Christopher protested.

"Whatever," Shiv said. "They still don't match." He offered Eric a handkerchief. "Better you than me. I faint when I bleed."

"You mean at the sight of blood," Elsa corrected.

"Of course not. That's silly," Shiv said. "I faint only when I bleed. Doesn't matter if I see it or not. It bloody hurts."

Christopher rubbed his hand down his face. "Bridges. We need THE bridge."

"What if it's not a thing?" Eric suggested.

Elsa frowned. "Bridges are things. We don't have any living bridges, do we?"

"We do," Eric said, "but that's not what I meant. What if it's a game?"

"You don't think Nana Romo meant that part? It doesn't really sound like something she'd put on her shopping list," Christopher protested. "Peanut butter. Cookies. A bridge."

Eric sighed. "No. A game. Bridge. Played with cards. Bidding and scoring."

Christopher looked confused. "You have games here?"

Elsa nudged him with her shoulder. "Just because all you've seen is doom, gloom, and end of the world doesn't mean we don't have fun sometimes. There's a bowling league on Tuesdays which gets a little awkward when the men wear bowler hats. Poker— most of the women wear body armor now— is on Friday nights. Tonight is bridge. Played with real bridges."

Now Christopher was truly confused. "How do you...?"

"Do you not play any games in the real world?" Shiv said. "We have cards. If you get the right cards, you take the trick. If you take the hand, then you win a bridge."

"You forgot about the cards changing and landscapes," Eric reminded him. "Bring your own fire extinguisher."

"Not exactly how we play, especially the fire extinguisher part, but I can run with that," Christopher said. "Where is it played?"

Elsa just rolled her eyes. "At the Bridge Club, of course." She smiled. "At least now we know where to go."

Everyone looked at Christopher.

NOT DEAD

After Christopher convinced them he couldn't possibly make them end up somewhere he knew nothing about,[139] they had started walking and were making good progress, just outside the city that hosted the Bridge Club. The road had changed over time from dirt to cobblestone to pavement. Eventually they had to walk on the side to avoid traffic. The fields had grown green, then developed sidewalks, fire hydrants, and houses. The skyline changed from endless horizon to booming city.

Then Eric swallowed a mosquito.[140]

He had been telling them stories about all his deaths when the mosquito flew right into his mouth. "I swallowed," he gagged. "I didn't mean to swallow. Tried not to swallow."

"Spit it back up," Shiv suggested.

"Too late," Eric grimaced. His face changed. "I didn't know mosquitoes could sting on the way down." In less than three minutes he was lying on the ground vomiting.

"Pizza." Shiv observed.

Elsa looked away. "Croissant with butter."

"Ice cream sandwich. Seriously, Eric, how much did you eat before this?" Christopher couldn't seem to look away no matter what Eric vomited up.

Eric was less amused and out of things to vomit, so he just dry heaved in Christopher's general direction. Christopher side-stepped the noxious air easily.

"I don't like this," Elsa said. "He's really sick."

"He'll likely die," Shiv said philosophically. "That **is** the thing he does, right?"

"But we're running out of time and he's not dead yet," Elsa fussed. "How long do we wait?"

---

[139] He could, if his imagination is good enough, otherwise there'd be no science fiction to speak of.

[140] Swallowing a mosquito isn't quite as common as following a fly.

Christopher looked at Eric. He was a pasty shade of yellow, his eyes sunk deep into his head. "I don't think he's going to make it much longer. The smell may kill him if the mosquito doesn't. Or the smell will kill us."

"I can hear you," Eric croaked. "A little sympathy? I'm dying here."

"Die a little faster," Shiv suggested. "We're on a timetable. Sympathy after saving the world."

Eric died in the middle of giving him a single-fingered salute.

"He couldn't even get all his fingers up," Elsa said sadly. "I feel terrible."

For once, Eric's body didn't disappear shortly after his death. It just lingered there, looking pained.

"Should we just leave him?" Christopher asked. "We can start walking and he'll catch up again."

Shiv shrugged. "He is dead. Hard to carry around a corpse."

Then Eric twitched.

"Maybe he's not dead yet." Elsa walked over to get a closer look. "Ugh, he smells dead enough."

"Yeah, but he smelled like that before he died," Christopher pointed out.

Eric sat up.

"Dude, you don't look good at all," Christopher grimaced. "Are you sure you don't want to stay dead?"

Eric reached for Elsa, who smacked him. "No. I already told you no."

Christopher reached for Elsa and pulled her back. "Um... maybe he really did die."

"What do you mean? He's moving."

"Don't you have zombies in your world?" Christopher mimicked Shiv perfectly. "I think he just turned into a zombie."

"How could he be a zombie? We're not zombies." Elsa peered more closely at Christopher. "Are we?"

Christopher pulled her back further as Eric lumbered to his feet. "I'm pretty sure we're not. We didn't swallow a mosquito that stung us on the way down."

"That's ridiculous," Shiv muttered. "You can't become a zombie by swallowing a mosquito." He backed up anyway. "Next you'll try to convince me that you can make dinosaurs out of mosquitos.[141]"

"You reincarnated as a pregnant female dragon," Christopher pointed out. "I'm pretty sure anything is fair game."

"But we need him! Alive him, not zombie him!" Elsa wailed. "He can't be undead. That's the worst thing he could be."

"Hope he can't hear you," Shiv said. "I may have fried him once, but that was for his own good. He might not like this show of affection." He kept his distance from everyone. "You're very hurtful people, you know?"

"Us? You say mean things all the time," Christopher said. "Why are you backing away from us?"

"Just in case," Shiv said. "We don't **know** the mosquito caused the zombie bit. If you act like him, I want a head start. I don't run very fast."

Eric was standing up but not moving after them. They all watched him as time ticked by.

"He seems fairly harmless," Elsa said.

"Until he eats one of us," Shiv added.

"We have to kill him," Christopher said.

The other two stared at him. "You're awfully fond of killing people lately," Elsa said. "Are you sure you're not one of those writers who kills everything when they're stuck for a plot?"

"I don't **have** a plot. Not the same thing as being stuck for one. He's dead anyway and may eventually want to eat us. We can't leave him, but we can't stay here. We have one hour," Christopher pointed out. "That's not a lot of time for him to regenerate or whatever he does."

---

[141] This is, of course, a ludicrous idea. No one would fall for it.

Everyone turned back to look at Eric. "How do you kill a zombie?" Elsa asked finally.

Christopher shrugged. "It depends on the type of zombie: fast, slow, inhumanly crazy-fast. Slow ones vary, but cutting off the head is usually a safe bet. Since he's not moving, I'm guessing he's not either version of fast."

They both stared at him.

"I don't read as much as I should," Christopher said defensively. "I do watch movies. I know how zombies die."

Shiv turned green. "Did I mention a distaste for the sight of blood?"

"You said it was only your own blood," Elsa reminded him.

"Yes, well, I've since changed my mind. No blood."

"He's dead. Pretty sure he doesn't bleed anymore." Christopher frowned. "Pretty sure."

"Pretty sure he's a zombie. Pretty sure he needs to die. Pretty sure he doesn't bleed and we need to cut his head off. Is there anything you are certain of?" Shiv snarked.

Christopher looked at Elsa. "I'm pretty sure I'm never going to love another woman like I love you."

"Then get a pet," Shiv suggested. "No sappy romantic scenes before the end of the world."

"Sorry," Christopher colored.

"Just didn't want to add my vomit to what Eric produced," Shiv shrugged away the apology. "I'll find something to cut his head off. If you get touchy, I may use it on you."

Eric had finally started moving. He shuffled to one side in an awkward circle, taking in his surroundings.

"He looks hungry. Did you bring any food? Small animals? Helpless babies?" Shiv was still backing up and looking around for anything to fight with. "Alright, the last bit was a tad callous. Edit that out, mentally.[142]"

---

[142]   The editor decided to not edit it out, literally.

"Out of food," Elsa gritted through the corner of her mouth. She'd picked up a large branch. "Don't think I can take his head off with this, either."

A woman ran into their clearing, holding a large knife. "Help me! I'm being chased by a …". Her words cut off as Eric grabbed her and took a bite out of her arm.

"Zombie," Shiv pointed out helpfully. "Guess I was a little late. Think it'd do any good to try to save her?" he asked Christopher.

"Usually a single bite is enough to infect a person," Christopher got a little too close, trying to get a good look, only to have Elsa yank him back.

"Can't believe she didn't see him." Elsa swallowed a few times, watching Eric. "He's a really messy eater."

"She had a knife." Christopher was edging forward. "She had a pretty big knife."

Elsa pulled him back. "You realize that Eric could eat you, too, right?"

"I'll just have to chance it. Worried about me?" Christopher asked hopefully.

"Gagging," Shiv said. "Really. That's absurdly nauseating. Worse than the zombie eating and mosquito vomit." He grabbed the branch from Elsa. "Try to not destroy the universe with your forbidden love before I get back."

"You might die," Christopher called out.

"Reincarnation," Shiv called back. "Possibly even heroic reincarnation. Added bonus of being spared the sight of you two making love eyes at each other while trying to pretend you're not. Death is better."

Eric was still chowing down hungrily on the unnamed woman, making sloppy, slurpy sounds. Shiv edged closer, looking between the knife and Eric, but Eric seemed to be a one-track eater. Using the branch, Shiv dragged the knife slowly closer to him.

"Got it!" he triumphed, holding it aloft.

Unfortunately, Eric chose that moment to let out a large belch and look around. When he saw Shiv, he got to his feet and wiped his arm across his mouth.

Shiv backed up. "I changed my mind. I'd rather not be a hero."

"You have the knife," Elsa called.

"Come on over. I'll give it to you," Shiv called back, still watching Eric. "Really. I'm alright with sharing, just this once."

"He's slow and a zombie. You can take him," Christopher encouraged.

"I'm slow and not a zombie. Fairly even odds there, if you ask me." Shiv bumped into a tree, took a moment to look behind him, and then started working his way around it backwards.

Eric seemed content to follow after him, occasionally emitting a burp so noxious Christopher and Elsa could smell it from their safe distance.

"C'mon, Eric. Fall on the knife like a good zombie." Shiv looked back at the other two. "This is boring, to be honest. Sure one of you don't want a go?"

As he looked back, Eric shambled forward. The girl he'd dined on also got to her feet, or what was left of them. Eric grabbed Shiv by the sleeve just as the girl started toward them.

"Hey, let go!" Shiv protested. "We're friends. Alright, traveling companions, but let go anyway. I'm not tasty. I was a dragon earlier. Probably give you indigestion. Shrimp, too. Maybe you're allergic to shellfish." He didn't look behind him this time. "A little help here."

Christopher started forward, but Elsa grabbed his arm and called out to Shiv, "You have both weapons." The branch thudded with fair accuracy at their feet.

Elsa sighed and handed the branch to Christopher. "Be careful."

He hefted the branch in his hand, holding back. "I don't think I reincarnate."

"I know." Elsa gave him a gentle shove. "I did say be careful. We're running out of time."

127

Christopher stumbled forward, nearly smacking into Shiv. "Sorry."

"Doesn't count as help if you knock me over. Think you can take one of them?"

Christopher shrugged. "Probably not, but I can distract her so you can take out Eric."

"Positivity. Good start." Shiv slashed out with the knife at Eric. "I've never taken a head off before. Should be easy, right?"

"Right," Christopher grunted as the branch connected with the zombie woman. "Piece of cake."

Shiv stabbed at Eric and the knife got stuck in his ribs. "No. Not cake." He tugged at the knife. "Not even pie." Eric started thrashing at him. "Maybe an entire side of beef. Poor choice of words, sorry." He tried to tug the knife free without getting bit. "Entire herd of beef." He finally pulled the knife free. "He's not cooperating."

"He's a zombie." Christopher knocked the woman's feet out from under her. "He's not supposed to cooperate."

"Now you tell me," Shiv grumbled. He suddenly darted forward, sliced the knife across Eric's throat, and pulled back.

Eric-zombie tried to hold his head to his neck, rather unsuccessfully.

"Where did **that** come from?" Christopher gaped at him.

"Pay attention to your zombie," Shiv chided. He gave another swipe and only Eric's spine was holding his head on his body. "I just remembered spending some time with ninjas of questionable morals in a past life.[143] Do you need help with that one?"

"If you don't mind." The female zombie had Christopher backed against a tree and he was holding her off with frantic pokes of the branch.

---

[143] Characters have a knack for suddenly developing talents readers had no idea they had. It shouldn't be easier to believe in zombies than in ninjas of questionable morals. (Unless it's just the questionable morals. That is a little hard to swallow.)

It took only a few minutes for Shiv to dispatch the female zombie as well. By the time he finished, Eric's body had disappeared.

"That was almost fun." He stabbed the knife into the ground a few times to clean it. "How long until he comes back?"

Christopher casually backed away from Shiv. "I don't know." He eyed the knife. "You don't feel any need to go on a killing spree or anything else you may have forgotten to tell us, right?"

Shiv looked at him. "Really? I kill a zombie I'm asked to kill and you think I'll go on a murderous killing spree. Is that how all writers think?"

Christopher shrugged. "I don't know many writers. I never make it to any of the writing events." He looked at the female zombie. "You did forget about the ninjas of questionable morals."

"Disadvantage to being reincarnated repeatedly in a short period of time."

Eric suddenly popped up right next to him, spitting repeatedly. "Do **not** let that happen to me again. I can still taste zombie in my mouth. I can still taste *human* in mouth." He scrubbed his tongue with the tail of his shirt. "Nasty. I thought burning while being wrapped up in psycho female was bad."

Elsa slipped her hand through Christopher's arm. "You're a terrible zombie killer."

"I know."

"It was still sweet to try to save me."

"I did save you." Christopher was affronted.

"Well," Elsa temporized, "technically, Shiv saved me."

Shiv made no attempt not to gloat. Christopher pulled away and made no attempt not to sulk. Eric pulled up a handful of grass, shoved it in his mouth, and made no attempt not to gag.

"So," Elsa said into the uncomfortable silence, "should we make it to bridge by eight?"

Christopher modified his glare after a glance at the knife Shiv was still holding. "I guess we'd better. But if you kiss him, I'm writing him dead without a resurrection when I get back to real life."

Shiv looked affronted. "You can't do that. I'm not even your character."

"I turned a roomful of characters into poop heads by accident. Intentional perma-dead for one sounds easy."

"Poor sport," Shiv said. Then he pointedly took several steps away from Elsa and started toward the city.

RAMEN NOODLES AND FAIRY GODMOTHERS

There was a huge crowd around the bridge table when they arrived, but all four playing seats were empty. People were packed so tightly that Christopher and Elsa held hands to stay together until a lightning bolt struck right between them.

"Fine," grumbled Christopher, releasing Elsa's hand. "Silly conventions."

Eric and Shiv immediately moved to either side of Elsa, increasing Christopher's scowl. "Just helping," Shiv assured him. "So you don't slip up to either side."

"Not me," Eric said. "I'm moving in on your woman while you're busy saving the world." When Elsa elbowed him, he grunted. "Alright, I'll wait until you die from saving the world and I'll comfort her."

Suddenly, Elsa pointed. "Isn't that Nana Romo?" She started pulling Eric and Shiv with her, leaving Christopher to follow.

"I don't like being a hero," Christopher muttered as he worked through the crowd, having trouble staying behind Elsa. "Villains have all the fun."

Nana Romo was giving a tube of something to a knight in full armor and scowled at Elsa when she interrupted. "I'm doing business, girl. Go away."

Elsa didn't leave. "I'll wait."

Nana Romo turned her back on Elsa and tried to continue her conversation. "Put a little bit in his food, but only a little. Don't mix it with lemons."

The knight turned the tube over in his hands. "Why not lemons? Will it heal him?"

"Heal him?" Nana poked the knight with the end of her cane, eliciting a loud clang. "He's an egg splattered into a million pieces. That's more like resurrecting the dead. It will taste like scalded turnips when you mix it with lemon juice. Grape is better."

"But how do I feed grape juice to an egg?" The knight looked ready to give the tube back.

131

"Not my concern!" Nana cackled. "You already bought it and no returns, no refunds. Now, off with you!" She swung her cane again. The knight hopped over the cane awkwardly, then clanked off to his horse. "Well?" Nana prompted Elsa.

"We're here. We made it."

The old woman scratched the end of her crooked nose with a long fingernail. "So?"

Elsa just stared. "So?" she screeched finally. "So?? We did your prophecy! We're here!" She looked ready to grab the cane and whack Nana Romo with it.

Christopher slipped between them. "Isn't this where I go home?"

"It's a prophecy, not a free trip for two to the Berhamas.[144]" Nana Romo was already walking away. "I just say the words. I don't make things happen."

"But what about me going home?" Christopher was now eying the cane.

Elsa stood next to him, fingertips almost brushing his before she pulled back. "What about my story?"

"I wouldn't mind a good, permanent death," Eric threw in.

"Why not?" Shiv shrugged. "I'd like a heart." Eric glanced sidelong at him. "What? It sounded more noble than asking for infinite riches and prosperity. I might reincarnate as a germ for that."

Eric let it pass.

"Look," Nana Romo planted her cane firmly in the ground. "I just do the prophecies. You can find your own way home," she jabbed at Christopher. "You've known how all along." She rolled her eyes at Elsa. "Don't look at me for your story. You already made one." She turned, started to walk away, then stopped, rummaging in the huge purse slung over her left arm. "Ah, yes." She turned and held something out to Shiv, who took it with a

---

144 The Berhamas are triangle-shaped islands where everything ever lost appears. There's especially an abundance of single socks, house keys, and homework pages.

puzzled expression that quickly turned to a disgusted one. "Your heart."

Shiv opened his fingers and let a raw heart fall to the ground, leaving his fingers bloody. "That is disgusting."

Nana Romo wiped her hands on her skirt. "Perfectly good heart. I was going to have it stewed with cabbage. Should've asked for the riches, boyo." She turned away.

"Wait," Eric stepped forward. "What about me?"

Nana Romo whacked him in the kneecap with her cane. "Best I could do is kill you myself, but it wouldn't be permanent. Make your own story or talk to your writer! Do I look like Sandy Klause?[145] Everyone thinks seers are magic fairies! Fix your own problems. I have a game to play." She slogged off through the crowd, occasionally laying about her with the cane to get people to move.

"I wish…" Elsa said.

Before she could finish, there was a flash of light and a tiny woman appeared. She had dark hair worn in loose curls, skin that drank in the sunset and held a faint sheen, and dark eyes that danced with laughter, wisdom, and a touch of mischief. Her gown was yellow silk, carefully slit to make room for gossamer wings. "My name is Margie. You look lost, my dear."

"We've come so far," Elsa said with a touch of a sob.

Christopher said nothing. Instead, he sat down to remove another rock from his shoe.

"Little disappointing," Shiv said diplomatically, trying not to shake any of the blood off his hand onto Margie.

Margie's huge eyes reflected Elsa's sadness. "I'm so sorry for your pain. Would you like me to fix it?"

Elsa looked hopeful. "Would you?"

"Could you?" Christopher stood, shoe still in hand.

Elsa wiped her eyes. Shiv made a point of not wiping his.

---

[145] Sandy Klause sells deeply discounted summer vacations.

Margie suddenly smacked Christopher so hard that he landed back on the ground. "Just because I'm a fairy doesn't mean I'm your fairy godmother.[146] Spoiled children, always wanting people to do things for you."

Christopher rubbed his shoulder where she hit him. "We just...".

"We just, we just," Margie mocked. "Solve your own problems. This isn't a fairytale. It's real, written life. Bother me again and I'll send a plot ninja[147] after you." There was another flash of light, then she vanished.

"So," Eric said into the silence that followed, "I guess I'm living forever."

Shiv looked down at his bloody hand. "I guess I'll ask for riches next time."

Elsa patted Christopher on the hand, then pulled back when distant thunder rolled. "You can still write my story."

"So all we have to do is get me back," Christopher said philosophically. "Maybe we should go watch the game and see if we can manage that."

Before anyone could move, a great vat of noodles in broth dropped from the sky, crushing a woman. A man sat inside the vat, bathing himself with a flesh-colored blobby fish, oblivious to the crowd. "Tameka!" a woman screamed. "He killed Tameka!"

"We might want to hurry up," Eric observed. "If that's not a sign of the end of the world, I'm not sure what is."

---

[146] Fairies left the Catholic church in droves, refusing to be godmothers, after girls started demanding bigger and grander wishes.

[147] Plot ninjas rewrite a plot so subtly that not even the characters remember the original plot line.

BRIDGE CLUB

Four beings sat at the bridge table: Tock, the being of non-heteronormative tendencies; Katrina, who still had a punk hair style and leather clothing; Kirkpatrick, wearing his sword; and Nana Romo, her cane looped over her right knee. The table was oddly shaped, like a square had been fused to a circle, with the four players sitting between the points. It was covered in a grassy surface and had moving streams, well-stocked lakes, and tiny living trees.[148]

Tock was currently in a genderless grey shape with blue edges.[149] Nana Romo was poring over a booklet and ignoring the other players unless they tried to talk to her. Then she whacked them with her cane without looking up. Katrina was pointedly ignoring Kirkpatrick. He was trying to ignore her as well, but was doing poorly at it.

It was five minutes to eight when Shiv, Eric, Elsa, and Christopher finally found a place near the front.

At one minute to eight, the sky was lit with all the colors of sunset: deep blues twirled with misty greens, pale oranges slicing across the edges, warm pinks in thick curls, and the faintest flare of light yellow.

Then the light disappeared.

For one full minute, it was pitch dark. The entire gathering was silent, as if in reverence for the ending of the day. Even Christopher resisted asking questions, somehow understanding the solemnity of the moment. Then stars twinkled to life in the darkness and strategically-hung lights flickered on, giving the entire area an otherworldly, fairytale look.

---

[148] Urban legend says the Bridge Table was originally created by the great world builder Tolkein as a place for one of his characters to practice fishing. Eventually the table was donated to the Bridge Club and has been there ever since.

[149] All shapes were genderless until two hundred years ago. At that time, they petitioned Character Court for genders in the misguided belief that genders would make them fit together better. The petition was granted and geometry and shape genders were created simultaneously. Few humans or shapes have understood the other since.

135

Nana Romo shuffled the deck of cards sitting in front of her, her bony hands seeming larger in the faint light. Kirkpatrick fiddled with a dagger, twirling it on its point until Katrina leaned over.

"I killed a man with one of those today. He took a very long time to die." Her voice carried clearly to the crowd as she leaned back in her chair and put her booted feet up on the table. "He did less to irritate me than you're doing right now."

Kirkpatrick scowled and put the knife away. "I find thee irksome and forsooth would call thee out, but the is game afoot and play is at hand. I shall abstain for the nonce."

Tock, shifted to the form of a mermaid, complete with long, flowing hair and shell accessories, ignored everything but the cards.

Nana Romo pushed the cards into a pile, then flicked the top one across the table. It landed perfectly in front of Kirkpatrick. When it settled, it changed into a small lake, complete with miniature fish.

"Bollocks," Kirkpatrick complained.

The next card landed in front of Katrina and changed into a mountain capped with snow. As Christopher watched, a small goat ran down the mountain, butted Katrina's hand, bleated, and frolicked away.

Katrina reached over, retrieved Kirkpatrick's dagger from the table, and stabbed at the mountain. Then she returned the dagger, tip damp with blood.

Tock acquired a deep ravine. There was a smattering of applause from the crowd around Christopher, although he had no idea why. Tock shifted into an eagle with long fingers at the end of its wings.

Nana Romo dealt herself a card that turned into a skyscraper, lit up with electric lights. Then she set the deck aside.

"What's going on?" Christopher asked Elsa. "I don't get how this works."

"Shhh." She put her hand on his arm and distant thunder boomed. Elsa removed her hand. "Just watch."

To the side, Eric and Shiv were making side wagers based on the cards already dealt.[150]

Kirkpatrick looked at his lake from every angle, even getting up from his seat to make a slow circuit around the table. Katrina tripped him as he passed and his hand went to the hilt of the sword at his side. Then he scowled and let it drop. "Much you have to make amends," he warned her. "But only after gaming ends."

Turning back to the table, he rolled two dice and dropped them. They rolled end on end, then turned into small workers with hardhats. The workers marched over to his lake and stood there, waiting. Kirkpatrick turned to Katrina and bowed. "Your turn, lady."

Katrina looked at her mountain, fingers steepled beneath her chin, for a long time. Then she leaned forward and rolled her dice.

One die turned into a small bundle, bound tightly in ropes. The other turned into a tiny female figure in a white toga.

Katrina picked up the female figure by her toga and dropped her none-too-gently on the mountain. Then she put the small bundle at the base of the mountain, looking pleased with herself.

"What is that?" Christopher whispered.

Elsa didn't shush him, but several others did. "Explosives. Just watch. You'll learn."

Tock didn't wait for Katrina's permission. He was now a maned lion, so he batted the dice across the table. One turned into a man wearing a hard hat, just like Kirkpatrick's had. The other turned into wood. Tock used one claw to guide the man toward his ravine, then put the wood in front of the worker. The sound of hammering and sawing immediately filled the air.

"Nicely done," Eric said approvingly. "As long as he doesn't fall off the edge."

---

[150] The betting for Bridge are even more complicated than the game itself. You can bet on which cards will be dealt, what each card will do, what each dice will do, who will flounce, who will win, who will lose, and who will act out of character. The last bet is the most risky and has the biggest payout.

137

"Rare," Shiv said. "Might sever a finger, though."

Nana Romo's dice turned into two small bundles. She put them both at the base of her skyscraper, then tapped the table.

Kirkpatrick dove beneath the table. Katrina put on sunglasses. Tock shifted into a metal safe.

The bundles exploded with a dramatic shower of fireworks, then the skyscraper folded in on itself before dissolving into a pile of rubble. Kirkpatrick slowly extricated himself from beneath the table.

"That's a gutsy move," Shiv approved. "Dangerous, but gutsy." Eric passed him some coins, which he pocketed.

The play was back to Kirkpatrick. He poked at his workers. One started digging near the lake. The other walked into the water and disappeared. There were bubbles for a minute, then nothing.

"Try my patience does this game;

Every play is all the same.

Luck has danced just out of hand;

With this play I barely stand."

Katrina rolled her eyes. "Could you be any more dramatic, you whiner?" She reached over for his dagger again and stabbed at her mountain. There was a brief, tiny scream. "I offer this virgin sacrifice in exchange for a bridge," she smiled.

A bridge appeared near her mountain. It landed directly on top of the pile of explosives, however, and was turned into a pile of rubble before Kirkpatrick could dive from his seat.

"Zuckerburg!" Katrina cursed, then stabbed the dagger back into the tabletop near Kirkpatrick. The chair she was sitting in immediately dumped her backwards. "Alright, sorry! I won't stab the table again." She righted the chair and sat back down. "Not a word," she warned Kirkpatrick.

Tock's man had built the framework for a bridge, but had run out of wood. Tock just curled up in its chair like a snake, eyes closed, and let the turn pass to Nana Romo.

Nana Romo poked at her smoking pile of rubble, but nothing happened. "Didn't see that coming," she muttered.

"Not a very good fortune teller," Eric noted. Shiv passed his coins back to him.

Nana Romo shuffled the cards again. Christopher leaned into Elsa. "Aren't we supposed to be doing something here?"

She shrugged, leaning into him as well. "I don't know what, though. Just that we needed to be here." Her arm slipped around his back.

Without thinking about it, Christopher kissed her, tasting vanilla on her lips.

The bridge table exploded.

FAVORING FIRE

Some say the world will end in fire
Some say in ice.
From what I know of desire
I hold with those who favor fire.
　　　　- Robert Frost "Fire and Ice"

... This is the way the world ends
Not with a bang but a whimper.
　　　　- T.S. Eliot "The Hollow Men"

Christopher felt as if he was on fire. His eyes burned. His skin was raw, even his clothing painful to the touch. His mouth was a dry wasteland. Then he realized he **was** on fire and dropped to the ground, rolling around in the dirt.

He wasn't the only one. There were dead and dying everywhere around him, but there were plenty of slightly injured as well. Once he wasn't actively on fire, Christopher ignored all of them. "Elsa?" His voice was a rough whisper. He didn't remember screaming, but his throat was raw. He swallowed and tried again. "Elsa, where are you?"

"Here." Her voice was almost as weak as his. "I... I can't...".

She was lying on the ground, head propped up against a tree. A long splinter of the table was sticking out from her ribcage about a foot. Her shirt was torn and bloody, but she didn't seem to have been burned.

"What happened?" Christopher crawled over to her, trying to not jostle her.

She answered the bigger question, not the smaller one. "We kissed again. The world exploded. Well, the bridge table.[151]"

---

[151]　The bridge table is just a world in miniature (or was), so she's right.

Christopher looked around them. Everywhere characters were screaming, or running, or burning, or bleeding. Or dead. "We did this?"

She tried to shrug, but it turned into a cringe of pain. "We kissed. The game exploded. Seems like it."

Christopher tried to get a better look at the jagged piece of wood. "You're bleeding. A lot."

Suddenly Eric and Shiv were next to them. "So, turns out you can trigger the end of the world with kissing. My mother is going to be so pleased to find out she was right." Shiv was holding the dagger that had been on the table. Eric had a bloody shovel.

"We didn't mean to," Christopher protested.

"Right. Just like most things that happen in history."

Elsa tried to push herself up to a sitting position. "A table exploded. Not the end of the world."

Eric hefted his shovel. "You haven't been looking around, have you? Total Armapocalypse."

Christopher looked at him blankly.

"Over there," he waved vaguely, "are zombies, vampires, and other monsters from mythology. On the other side of us is an overwhelming alien armada. The machines are advancing from the front."

"Then we'll go back." Elsa had managed to push herself to a fully sitting position. "Help me to my feet?"

"Oh, back is best of all. Back behind us are the gnomes. Millions of garden gnomes, all ready to get revenge for years of sitting in gardens with manure on their feet." Eric seemed almost cheered by this.

"I need a weapon," Christopher got to his feet. "Keep her safe. I'll be right back."

As he ran through the crowds, he saw one lone bee weave drunkenly above the characters, then drop to the ground, dead. Plants started withering around it. He looked around frantically.

Kirkpatrick and Katrina were squaring off. He had his sword out, point already bloody. She had a thick piece of wood she was holding like a bat.

"Be thou still, mercurial bit of womanhood!" Kirkpatrick bellowed. "Thou hast beggared my patience far too long."

Katrina side-stepped the sword point easily and swung at him, missing entirely. "You're a self-important dandy who can't even play fairly at bridge. Might as well die." She sounded bored.

Christopher tried to move between them, but they just moved to one side and continued hurling insults. "Guys, end of the world. We need help. Hello?" He managed to distract both of them just enough that Katrina smashed Kirkpatrick upside the head just as he ran her through. Each looked at the other in shock.

"What have you done?" Katrina sank to the ground with the sword still entrenched in her ribs. "Why did you do that?"

Kirkpatrick weaved unsteadily toward Katrina, one hand to his head where blood was gushing through his fingers from his cracked skull. "I fear that death has found its way to us both, fair lady, and by the hand of who we loved the most."

Christopher couldn't say a word. He just stared at them both. "But I... I didn't...". Guilt choked off the rest.

Katrina managed to pull the sword out, blood bubbling out from between her ribs. "Where's Shiv? He'd probably say something about karma right now."

[Kirkpatrick] "Betwixt your words, because you cried,
My hopes for love have thus here died.
My sword has sipped a drink so fair
That, should I die, I do not care.

You could not wait, you could not see,
The banter betwixt her and me.
I call a curse upon your soul
And her who you most wish to hold.

And so I die; my eyes do fade.

142

Without the love of this fair maid.
Too long to tell her I did wait;
Too soon to tell her is too late."

Kirkpatrick dragged himself to Katrina in heroic measure and pulled her to his chest. Both were dead in a matter of minutes.

The sky darkened further, but Christopher didn't notice. "I don't understand. I don't understand any of this. I never studied history or literature. I don't know a lot of big words. I just wanted to write a story and fall in love." He picked up the sword and tried to wipe off the blood on the grass. "I just want to go home, but first I'm going to save Elsa." He started to turn away, then turned back. "I'm sorry. I really am."

He trotted back to the other three, dodging a five-foot tall snail, three talking bears, and a living balderdash. He wasn't sure which were good guys and which were bad guys, so he avoided them all.

Shiv and Eric were pouring salt on another large snail when he arrived. It would dissolve partially, then reform. "Hydra slugs,[152]" Eric explained. "Nasty things since they learned to steal shells. Can't get salt on them fast enough to kill them before they regenerate."

Christopher kicked a garden gnome that was trying to gnaw his shoe. It went flying, but he felt his pinky toe break with the impact. "Do the shells break?"

Eric looked at Shiv. Shiv looked at Eric. "I guess they do."

All three of them swung at the shell in unison. Large cracks formed, then the shell fell apart. Eric poured salt on the slug again and it dissolved entirely.

"How do you know which creatures to attack?" Christopher asked, stomping on another garden gnome. This one exploded, then crumbled into dust.

---

[152] Not to be confused with hydration slugs, which are quite useful in the garden.

"If it bites you, hits you, scratches you, or in any other way acts aggressively, kill it," Shiv suggested.

Elsa was still leaning against the tree. At least the tree wasn't acting aggressively yet. "How are you doing?" Christopher kept an eye out as he crouched by her.

She didn't answer immediately. "Oh, I'm fine," she finally said. "I seem to have a little splinter, but I can wait to take care of it."

Before Christopher could respond, a multi-limbed metallic creature skittered around the tree. He couldn't see any eyes— or head, really— but the creature seemed to immediately hone in on Elsa.

Christopher got to his feet, holding the sword between him and the Excessopod. He didn't think it would do much good against a metallic creature, but he didn't have anything else and Eric and Shiv were both busy fighting a rain cloud. He'd process that one later.

He lifted the sword anyway and put his body between the Excessopod and Elsa. The creature advanced in short, tentative bursts. Christopher tripped over a root and fell backwards, just missing Elsa.

Out of nowhere, a pegicorn rammed into the Excessopod and sent it flying into the air. It landed in the top of Elsa's tree. The tree wrapped limbs around it and held it securely, no matter how much the creature thrashed its legs.

The pegicorn whinied and backed away from Christopher, but dipped its nose to Elsa. "Thank you," she breathed weakly. The pegicorn spread its wings and launched itself into the sky.

Christopher dropped the sword. He wasn't doing any good with it anyway. Eric and Shiv were fighting back to back, handily dispatching a small bevy of snorkles and a larger weeping fairy. Tock galloped through with Tuck right behind it. Tock knocked things down and Tuck buried them. Tick was nowhere to be seen.

Elsa took Christopher's hand. "You need to go home."

"I can't," he protested. "You're hurt. I can find something to save you."

144

"I'm dying," she corrected him gently. "I don't think you can stop dying, Christopher. Not unless you write it."

He gritted his teeth together. "I can try. I'm a writer, right?"

She tried to grab his arm. "No. You can't try here. You might ruin everything. You might die. You might..." Her fingers tightened momentarily around his arm, then slowly released.

Christopher just stared. She wasn't moving. She wasn't breathing. He knew she didn't have to breathe, but this was different. Just like the first time he'd encountered Eric, he knew.

She was dead.

He gently took her arms and placed them over her body, trying to make it look natural and failing terribly. He brushed a single braid away from her face and tried to clean a smudge of dirt from her cheek.

Then he cried.

He cried for the beautiful character he had created who had become so much more than he'd created. He cried for the amazing woman he'd fallen in love with and the knowledge that he'd never found anyone just like her in real life. Yes, she was like bits and pieces from others, but he'd taken all his favorite pieces and put them in her. He cried for all the characters dying just so some hack writer like him could feel like he was creating, when all he was really doing was destroying.

When he had no more tears to cry, he scrubbed a hand across his face, retrieved the sword, and stood, slamming the point of the sword deep into the ground. "No. I do not accept this. I do not." For the first time he could remember in his twenty-five years, he felt passionately about something, even if it was something he had no power over. "She is **not** dead."

Everything around him went still as his words echoed throughout the battlefield. Fighters froze on both sides. The sky darkened further and the air grew chill. Then the ground opened up beneath him and sucked everything inside.

PARLOR TRICKS

Christopher managed to scramble to the edge of the hole and grab the tree that Elsa was leaning against, but the hole kept widening. He and Elsa fell into the hole in a curious slow motion. He knew they were falling, but he could still see the entire battlefield.

The hole extended outward and Eric and Shiv were pulled in. Then further and Nana Romo, Tock, Tick, and Tuck all tumbled inside. Soon there was nothing left but the hole, which kept growing.

Elsa stirred beside him, her brown eyes suddenly open. "Oh no. Christopher, what did you do?"

For a moment he couldn't respond. "You're alive?" he breathed at last, more query than statement.

She grabbed his arms, face intense. "What. Did. You. Do?"

He finally registered the falling beings around him. "I…" he licked his lips. "I said you weren't dead."

Elsa took in a sharp breath. "You can't do that. It's a plot hole." She looked around them. "It's a huge plot hole." She'd been regaining her color, but now it drained from her face completely. "You may have destroyed everything."

Christopher rubbed at his arms. The air was growing colder by the second. "I just didn't want you to be dead. I didn't say, "resurrect her" or anything."

"Oh, Christopher, you impulsive, crazy writer. You don't have to say that. What you say becomes so. You just uncreated. You can't uncreate. If you had recreated me alive, then it might've been okay.[153] You uncreated my death. That's such a big plot hole… it might destroy us all."

Nana Romo was determinedly swimming toward them, a scowl on her pinched face. "What did you do, boy? What have both of

---

[153] Considering Frankenstein's monster and every zombie novel ever written, maybe not.

you done? All you needed was to go back home and instead you are going to destroy everything."

Christopher reached for Elsa's hand. She pulled away, then allowed it. "I couldn't live with her dead and no one else is giving me any answers. She is my answer. So I wanted her back." He looked at Elsa, then back at Nana Romo. "I didn't know this would happen, but I'm not sorry she's back. You can keep giving me a hard time or we can fix it. Help me, without any weird prophecies, any vague answers," he ducked as she swing her cane at his head, "and without hitting me! I'm tired of being hit."

"You have a lot of nerve, writer. You think I'm going to help you?"

"Yes." Christopher looked around. They were falling faster or it was more noticeable. "I think you will. It's the only thing that will save us."

"Us?" Nana Romo spit out the word.

"Yeah, us. You're in this hole, too, lady."

Eric and Shiv swam up to them. "Nice day we're having," Eric observed. "End of the world is getting a little boring. Any chance we could speed it up a bit?"

"Yeah, boring, this falling without anything happening," Shiv agreed. "Fighting was more fun. What are we doing?" He back-pedaled as Nana Romo swung at him. "Sorry. I'm not into contact sports."

Christopher locked eyes with Nana Romo. "We're saving the world. You in?"

The two men looked at each other. "May as well. We don't seem to be doing anything else." Shiv spoke for both of them. "Any idea when we'll be doing something?"

Elsa grimaced. "The plot hole is going to close, no matter what we do. That's about the only thing I do know for certain. I don't know anyone who's come out of a plot hole to talk about it, so I don't know what happens." She shrugged. "We get to play this one by ear."

Eric gave her a cheerful smile. "Did we have a plan before this? I'm a pantser,[154] myself. Just let the cards fall where they land."

Nana Romo hit him with her cane. "Are you all crazy? I'm not a gardener. I'm an architect![155] Of course we need a plan. We need a prophecy. We need a list."

Elsa snorted. "The last time we had a prophecy, it led us here. Did you ever do your grocery shopping?"

"No, but…"

"No 'buts'," Christopher said firmly. "We don't need an outline. We need a beginning and an end, and we need to know our roles. We're boopers.[156] We don't follow a game plan. The game plan follows us. I think we stopped moving."

Nana Romo didn't look pleased, but Elsa did. That was enough for Christopher. "So, now we need to get you all back to your world and me back to mine. That should be doable, right?"

"How long did you say you've been trying to get back to your world?" Shiv asked nonchalantly.

Christopher looked a bit sheepish. "About thirty-five thousand words." At Shiv's look, he grumbled. "What? I think better in words than time here. I can see the words better than the people and places."

Elsa blinked. "What did you just say?"

"He said he loses track of time around you," Eric offered helpfully.

"Time stands still when he's in your presence," Shiv added.

"**Not** helping," Elsa glared at both of them. "Words, Christopher. You said you can almost see the words."

---

[154]   Pantser: someone who writes without an outline or plays things by ear. In Eric's case, may also refer to pulling someone's pants down around the ankles.

[155]   Gardener: another word for a pantser (one who lets things develop naturally). Also, someone who grows plants.
Architect: someone who plans every last detail of a book. Alternately, someone who designs buildings. Nearly as hated by contractors as writers are by characters.

[156]   Boopers: yet another word for a pantser. By spending no time doing outlines, pantsers have plenty of time to create new words. Also members of the Betty Boop fan club.

Christopher nodded. "I can see how many words have passed like some people know how much time has passed. I never thought about it before this because no one asked, but I can see how many words pass when we travel, when we talk... that's a huge word sink, by the way. Travel, not so much."

"Great. He can see how many words it takes to get from 'start of Armageddon' to 'end of Apocalypse'. Very nice parlor trick." Shiv shook his head. "Can we get back to the game plan?"

Out of nowhere, the judge from the courtroom appeared, tail wagging eagerly. "Did you say 'parlor trick'? Do you have a parlor trick, now? I've been waiting to see one. I knew you had to have one." He still looked as Christopher had left him, human face on hot dog body with a tail. "Judge Ental," he introduced himself to Shiv, Eric, and Nana. "You can call me Melvin since we're not in court." He looked back at Christopher, tail still wagging. "Just one parlor trick?"

"Um," Christopher temporized. "You just generated eighty-five words of useless, interrupting side story?"

The judge tried to clap his paws together, which made him look like an over-eager seal. "Oh, very nice! I am so glad I got to see your parlor trick, even if it took the end of the world to get to that point."

"I'm never understanding this place," Christopher muttered in an aside to Elsa. "Never."

She patted his arm with a smile. "You don't have to understand us. You make us what we are, you and all those other writers."

Christopher face-palmed. "That gives me very little hope for saving us and no hope at all for saving the human race. We need facts. We need to know what we know."

Melvin's tail stopped wagging. "Best way to do that's in a courtroom. Good thing you know a judge."

"But we don't have a courtroom," Christopher pointed out.

"No, but we have a writer," Elsa pointed out.

Christopher frowned at her. "The last time I created something, it almost killed me, remember? I'm out of coffee."

Baristas appeared out of nowhere, each holding a different coffee drink, tea, or soda. Two even brought energy drinks. They weren't generic characters, either. Each was a fully realized personality, from the bubbly college student permanently hyped on her own wares to the older coffee maven who not only knew how to make every coffee drink from memory, but could tell exactly where every coffee bean came from.

"Did I do that?" Christopher frowned again. "I don't feel any differently. Shouldn't I be exhausted if I created that many characters?"

Shiv took the nearest tea. "Of course you didn't do that. You live in a world where coffee shops are on almost every corner. We live in a world where coffee shops are in almost every chapter. They probably all got sucked in with us."

Eric took a coffee and sipped. Nana Romo chased a male barista with an espresso, trying to hook him with her cane, but he wasn't letting her get anywhere near him.

"Plenty of caffeine, Christopher. Time to make us a courtroom," Elsa said. "Let's find out what we know."

Christopher sighed. "This place is so weird."

Elsa just grinned at him again. "Pot, kettle," she reminded him. "You write us. Besides, you said that already. No one likes a repetitive writer.[157]"

He took her hand, closed his eyes, and concentrated.

---

[157] Untrue, based on writers who make a very nice living rewriting the same plot in different books.

CHAPTER BREAK

The courtroom that formed around them was indistinct at first, with only the jury box and witness box being clearly defined. Even the outer walls were vague, nebulous forms of mist and smoke, more suited to a horror story than a legal drama.[158] Christopher frowned as he opened his eyes. "Will this work?"

Melvin shook his head. "We need a real courtroom to find out any real facts. I don't think this would pass as a courtroom."

Elsa squeezed Christopher's hand. "You can do it. Just remember what you did when you had to make everyone in court. You have the big picture, sort of. Focus on one area at a time and fill it in. You can do this."

Christopher took a swig of an energy drink, then a deep breath. He focused on the judge's seat, making it a massive marble affair with a soft chair for the judge and a stone gavel. He added a glass of water in the corner of the table and a seal on the front with the words "Justice -- Fairness -- Honesty" in a circle around a hot dog. The judge looked pleased. "Nicest place I've ever had."

He expanded the juror box until he could clearly see each of the twelve seats. The foreman's seat was a little bit larger than the other seats, with a thick cushion to make it a little more comfortable. The foreman gave him a grateful look and settled into the seat. The other jurors immediately began complaining.

Christopher was sweating and breathing heavily. "Unless you want to be the foreman, stop complaining. Random jurors almost never die[159] and they get to sit back and relax during most scenes. He deserves a nice chair." That shut them up. He made each chair individually, giving one a slight rip in the right corner, another a stain where an earlier juror had broken an ink pen all over the

---

[158] There are legal dramas that are also horror stories, but they are rarely set in mist- and fog-enshrouded courtrooms. The one exception is *Ghostly Love in the First Degree*, which meshed so many genres together that it was unmarketable.

[159] This was a flat-out lie, since random jurors die all the time, but it served its purpose.

seat. The jurors jostled with each other over the seats as well, then finally settled down and sat.

Christopher changed the witness box into a large, comfortable, wooden affair with a bench seat. He added a cushion, but Elsa elbowed him. "Witnesses don't get to be very comfortable."

The judge nodded in agreement, so he reluctantly removed the cushion. He added another cup of water and a microphone. Elsa nodded in approval.

He continued with the defense table, the prosecution table, and spectator seating. He went through both energy drinks and most of the coffee before he finished. He felt wrung out and wired at the same time, but he didn't feel like he was going to fade away to nothing or pass out.

"Good job!" Judge Ental enthused. "I can work with this. Now, we just need the right people."

The bailiff appeared next to Christopher and put him in handcuffs so quickly Christopher had no time to stop him. "What are you doing? Let me go!"

"It's the job, sir," the bailiff said respectfully. "If you're going to be the defendant, you need to be cuffed."

"But I'm not the defendant! I'm… a witness, maybe. Or an attorney."

Now the judge was shaking his head. "Do you have a law degree, son? You can't practice law in my courtroom without a law degree. I know writers have all sorts of loopholes, but we can't use that one here. You haven't even finished school. Don't make me find you in contempt of court. It would pain me. You have to be the defendant. It's the only way this works."

"Alright," Christopher conceded petulantly, "but do we need the cuffs?"

The bailiff gave him a baleful look and picked up a crochet hook. "Just doing my job, sir."

Again Christopher yielded, although this time begrudgingly.[160] "Fine. The cuffs stay. Just don't bring...".

"Sorry I'm late, Your Honor," a nasal voice interrupted. "I was held up by a garden gnome."

It was the prosecuting attorney, still looking about as happy as an angry elephant. Christopher groaned. "Anyone but her. Please?"

She gave him a haughty look. "I'm the only prosecuting attorney not currently written into an active scene. Most of *them* didn't get sucked into your moment of irresponsibility. You're stuck with me."

Christopher sighed and Elsa gave him a beseeching look. "Fine. Is everything set up for this, then?" He downed a cup of tea by accident and nearly spewed it out all over Shiv. "Sorry. I don't like tea."

"Can't expect you to have good taste in everything," Shiv sniffed. "So far, women and... no, that's it. Good taste in women."

Elsa blushed and Christopher grumbled. "Right here listening. Can you flirt with someone else?"

"That wouldn't bother you as much," Shiv pointed out. "So, no."

The bailiff pulled out a half-finished quilt, set it on his chair, then stood and cleared his throat. "Order in the court. All rise. The honorable Judge Melvin Ental presiding. You may be seated."

Everyone sat, including the judge. "We're here to find out the facts surrounding the curious case of the plot hole. Is the prosecution ready with her first witness?"

The attorney smoothed her skirt. "We are, Your Honor. We call Christopher Cullum to the stand."

Christopher started to sit down, but the bailiff shook his head. "Swear in, sir. We still have to follow protocol."

---

[160] The overuse of adverbs in this section caused two members of the Stephanos Rey Party to resign office.

The bailiff held out a leather-bound copy of *War and Peace* for Christopher to put his hand on. "Do you swear to tell the truth as your point of view sees it, the whole truth that you are currently privy to, and nothing but the truth unless you're written to tell a lie?[161]"

"That's not how it goes," Christopher protested. "And it's not how you did it last time."

"That's how it goes here for this time, sir. We're not in your world. That's the whole point, isn't it?"

Christopher put his hand on the book. "I do so swear, no matter how crazy I think this whole thing is."

"No extemporizing," the bailiff chided. "No one said any of this will make sense until the final chapter. The best books don't."

"Somehow," Christopher muttered, "I don't think this will ever go down as one of the best books."

"Perhaps not, sir, but it's best to go on believing just in case, don't you think?"

Christopher had nothing to say to that.

The prosecuting attorney stood in front of the witness box, fixing her lipstick. She completely ignored Christopher, taking her time carefully filling her upper lip in with vivid red, then her lower. Only when she had blotted her lips and applied a bit of shine over them did she look up at the witness box. "Oh, sorry, have you been waiting?"

"End of the world, but take your time," Christopher muttered.

The stenographer, the same poor woman with ears, arms, and little else, said, "Speak clearly, please."

Christopher flushed, but just waited.

The attorney glanced at her notes, which had appeared in her hands as if they'd always been there. "So, Christopher— you don't mind me calling you Christopher, do you?— what do you

---

[161] Telling a lie on the witness stand, even if written to tell a lie, is still perjury. As long as it's not perjury, it will be in the novel.

know about the plot hole that we're currently falling into and why did you decide to cause the end of the world?"

Melvin— Judge Ental— gave her a stern look that went much better with his sad-faced sixty-year-old man face than it had with his dog face. "One question at a time. No leading the witness. No assumption of facts."

The attorney gave him a frosty look. "Of course, Your Honor. Just the first question, then. What do you know about the plot hole we're currently falling into?"

Christopher cleared his throat and looked out into the audience for Elsa. He found her immediately, eyes on him, projecting so much support that he could almost see the word floating across the air to him. He took a deep breath, let it out slowly, and answered carefully. "Apparently when someone is brought back to life, it's an undoing, not a creation, so it causes a plot hole. It must be a pretty big one, because this plot hole is taking longer to close than the last one. Although we did stop moving. Maybe it closed and we don't know it."

The attorney latched onto one fact immediately. "So you've caused plot holes before?"

"Only once," Christopher assured her. "I only said the words, 'plot hole'. One appeared, then it closed up in less than a minute. I guess they take longer when they're created by accident."

"Save theories, please," the attorney cautioned him. "That's really the jury's job. Your job here is to provide facts, although," she turned to the judge, "are you sure I can't try him for undisciplined use of a plot hole, poor planning, and bad execution?"

The judge was sniffing at something in his hand. He put it down sadly. "Not the same sniffer. No, you may not prosecute him. He may be our best hope. Besides, he did a parlor trick for me. I haven't seen you do any parlor tricks."

The attorney grimaced and turned back to Christopher. "Alright, so you reversed death and caused a plot hole. Was there anything different about the person whose death you reversed? Intense hatred, perhaps?"

"Definitely not! I don't hate her. I love her." Christopher frowned. "Intense hatred is definitely out."

The juror box was buzzing like a nectar-drunk bee and all the jurors were talking excitedly amongst themselves. Eventually the judge had to bang his gavel— a real gavel— to get them to quiet down.

"Intense love is as strong as intense hatred," the attorney informed Christopher. "So you made a plot hole with intense feeling." She looked at the judge. "That has to be significant. May I speak directly to the jury?"

The judge nodded his assent. He was trying to lick something off the end of his nose and finding his tongue far too short.

"Members of the jury, I would ask that you pay particular attention to this fact: the plot hole was created with great feeling. When the plot hole was created with mere intention, it closed in less than a minute. When the hole was created with great feeling, it has stayed open, thus far, nearly an hour. It is, as yet, unclear if the fact that it was likewise created by uncreating is relevant."

Christopher dozed off in the witness box in the middle of her speech. It had been a very long day with lots of walking with little rest. He wasn't used to walking much and the caffeine crash was starting to get to him again. He startled awake when the bailiff tapped him on the shoulder. "Huh? Wha? I was just..." he wiped sleep mucus from the corners of his eyes, losing his train of thought. "I was doing something else. Not sleeping. What did you say?"

The attorney was pinch-faced again. "I asked you— three times, no less— who you sent into a plot hole the first time?"

Christopher frowned, trying to remember that morning. It had been so long ago and he had met so many characters since then. "She wanted to be a serial killer and knew that I could somehow write her into a story. She killed someone to demonstrate. That was disturbing."

"Yes, yes," the attorney made no attempt to hide her impatience. "But her name?"

"Chris!" It suddenly came to him. "She said we had the same name, almost. Her name was Chris."

As if his words summoned her, Chris appeared next to him in the witness box. The bailiff stood hastily and handcuffed her as well. Then he held out a large tome of *The Count of Monte Cristo*.

Chris looked around her, ignoring the bailiff. "Oh, people. How nice! And you, the writer! Did you change your mind about writing me? I'd be a good serial killer. I would. Did you, huh? Did you?"

The bailiff interrupted her. "You're in court, miss. Not really the best place to talk about killing. You need to swear in, if you would." He looked back to the quilt he'd nearly finished, longing in his eyes. "If you don't mind, put your hand on the book?"

Chris complied in a distracted manner. She was still faceless and her hair changed randomly at rapid intervals.

"Do you swear to tell the truth as your point of view sees it, the whole truth that you are currently privy to, and nothing but the truth unless you're written to tell a lie?" It was exactly what the bailiff had said to Christopher.

"Oh, I do, yes!" Chris said excitedly. "Does this mean I'm a character now and I get words and everything? Maybe a description? If I do, what point of view should I use? Do you think I could get written to tell lies? It's not as good as being a serial killer, but it's more memorable than just being a Chris." She turned to Christopher again. "No offense. You're still different because you have a full name. I don't. I'm just Chris. That has to be the most generic, boring name ever."

The jurors lifted their scorecards: 8 8 3 7 8 9 6 10 8 7 9 8.

"See? They mostly agree." Chris looked at the juror who'd given her a 3. "I bet your name is Chris." The juror blushed and dropped her scorecard, fading back into obscurity. "See what I mean?"

The attorney cleared her throat. "Apparently Chris is also a name that leads to mindless sidetracks, random drivel, and useless information, in short **or** long form. May we proceed?"

Chris didn't look remotely embarrassed. "Did I interrupt something? That's great. More character development. I really like you," she asided to Christopher. "Interesting things always happen around you."

The attorney pounced on that. "Speaking of interesting things, do you remember getting sent into the plot hole?"

"Oh, is that where we are? I thought maybe I just got written into a corner or left in a book without any scenery written for it. Totally wasn't holding that against you," she asided to Christopher again. "It was still the most interesting thing to happen to me all day until now."

The attorney gave a melodramatic sigh that didn't fit well with her appearance. "If you could **please** stick to the task at hand? Do you remember getting sent here?"

"Oh, yes. I remember. I was talking to Christopher and his nice girlfriend," she looked into the spectators, "oh, yes, the one out there. Hi! Remember me? We met earlier today and you told him to say 'plot hole'? Thank you for that! Really. No hard feelings."

"And," the attorney interjected, breaking a pen in frustration and getting ink all over her nice clothing, "what happened when you fell into the plot hole?"

"Well," Chris started, getting a vague look as she thought back, "at first nothing. I mean, I sort of knew I was falling, but it didn't feel like falling, so I kept trying to talk to Christopher. Then it closed."

"The plot hole closed."

"Yes, that's what I said. I was falling, then it closed."

"What happened when it closed?"

Chris looked around until she found the bailiff. "Could I get a drink? Maybe water with a little lemon? I'm parched and I really don't want to take Christopher's water, but I don't know how much more talking I can do without something to drink. I'm guessing wine is right out, so water would be fine, if you could."

The bailiff stood and set aside his quilt carefully. He had nearly finished and was working a delicate lace trim. "Of course." He brought her a cup of water that appeared out of nowhere, lemon floating near the top.

Chris drank down the entire cupful, set it down, then picked it up and drained it again. "Oh, better. Except I need a bathroom. May I go use a bathroom?"

It was the judge's turn to sigh. "We'll take a ten minute recess for bathroom breaks. Please return promptly."

Christopher was trying to see how Chris's cup had refilled (without dumping it out on himself) when Elsa settled in next to him. "Do you think this is helping?"

He looked back at her. She looked tired, but she'd been awake as long as he had, except when she was dead. "Do characters get tired?"

"Um, yes. If you write it. Do you think this is helping?" she repeated.

"I don't know," he admitted. "But it doesn't seem to be hurting. I don't know what else to do."

"Neither do I," she sighed. "Keep at it. Maybe something will happen." She got up to return to her seat, then turned back to him. "I love you, Christopher. I'm proud of you, too. There's more to you than I think either of us realized."

He blushed. "I love you, too, Elsa, but I've loved you for a long time. At least three days. You're definitely more than I imagined or created."

She leaned in to kiss his cheek and the entire courtroom shook. "Er, sorry. Guess I should get back to my seat."

Christopher watched her return to her seat. Eric and Shiv were sitting on either side of her, but they seemed to be behaving. The dagger Elsa had somehow brought in with her may have influenced their choice.

159

"So, this court thing, fun, isn't it?" Chris had returned to sit next to him and the bailiff was recuffing her. "I've never had the chance to do fun things like this. I think it would be even more fun to be a serial killer and get to be tried in court for killing many times. Can you imagine what a scene that would be?"

Christopher sighed and rested his head on the witness table. "I can."

Chris didn't take a hint and continued to chatter until the attorney returned and asked her to please shut up. Then she was silent for nearly twenty seconds before whispering to Christopher, "That was so rude."

The bailiff stood and announced the judge's return, then went back to his quilt. The judge settled himself and nodded to the attorney.

"You were about to tell us what happened when the plot hole closed," the attorney reminded Chris. "Do you think you could do that now?"

"Oh, of course! I remember it exactly, except that it wasn't very exact. It was more general in a sort of 'huh, that happened' way. Do you know what I mean?" She didn't wait for a response, but plowed on. "It was like one moment I could still see the outside, then I couldn't. That's the only real difference. I'm not exactly sure when it happened only because at the time I was looking at my arm. I have freckles on my arms, you see, and I was counting to see how many freckles I had right that second."

"You were counting your freckles?" The attorney's mouth had dropped open, giving her an unfortunate resemblance to a monkey.

"Yes. I had forty-three on one arm and forty-four on the other. I was trying to figure out why there was an odd number and how I could get one back on the arm that was missing one. Then I realized I couldn't see out the hole any longer and it was really quiet. So I looked up and it was closed."

"Finally," the attorney muttered under her breath.

"Louder, please," the transcriptionist warned.

"Then what happened?" the attorney asked, much louder.

"Oh, nothing. I just stayed there, waiting. I mean, I did other things. I didn't have anything to eat or drink and I didn't seem to need the bathroom, which was good, because there wasn't one. There wasn't anyone else, either. But that's all. I was just there. Nothing else."

"Nothing scary or dangerous? Nothing bad?" The attorney had to raise her voice to be heard over the rising volume of whispers from the audience.

"No. I guess being bored is bad, but I've been bored for a long time, so I'm used to it. There was just nothing."

Now the jury was whispering, too. Even the bailiff had looked up from his quilt. The judge finally had to bang his gavel again. "Order. Order!"

"No more questions for this witness, Your Honor," the attorney said over the quieter murmurs. "She can be dismissed."

"Oh, can I stay, please? This is the most excitement I've ever had and if you send me away I'll just go blend in with the audience and maybe never have another chance to say things and have anyone hear them. Or maybe I'll just stop being. I was a little worried about that before I was summoned. It was hard to keep being."

The attorney had been looking over her notes, but now she looked up. "What do you mean?"

"I mean, there wasn't anything else. Just the emptiness. I think it was unmaking me, somehow. I know I lost freckles, because I only have 37 on one arm and 36 on the other. I still don't know where that one off is, but there were more when I first fell into the plot hole."

The muttering rose up again from the spectators crowded into the viewing area. It seemed to Christopher that everyone he'd met was in that crowd, but the crowd was getting smaller. Some were still well-defined, like Elsa, Shiv, and Eric, but some were hard for him to make out. It looked like Ellie was sitting in a private box and the smoking man was only fuming slightly in a dark spot right in the middle of the courtroom. Nana Romo scowled at him from a corner and he hastily looked away.

"Your Honor?" The attorney seemed at a loss. "I don't have any more questions. I don't know what to do with this information."

Judge Ental looked over to the juror box. "What say you, foreman? Do you have any verdict?"

"Not yet, Your Honor." The foreman stood, holding a cap in his hands that he twisted around and around. "We would like to confer, if we could?"

The judge nodded. "But hurry. I have a feeling we're on a time limit." He got to his feet. "Another recess. I would recommend staying where others can see you. We'll return in fifteen minutes and decide where to go from there." He left the bench and took three of the four steps toward his chambers, then seemed to think better of it and sat down next to the bailiff. "Lovely quilt."

"Do you like it?" The bailiff's voice was smaller, less imposing, when he wasn't in official status. "It's for the baby character that got abandoned about twenty-three pages ago. It was off-camera, but all of us at the station are caring for her while we wait to see if she gets her own book later."

The judge tsked. "Sad the way that happens. I understand when it happens to us; we're old. But a baby has so much potential! Never makes sense to abandon a baby character."

Elsa came back up to sit next to Christopher. "I hope the jury saw something I didn't. There weren't any real solutions in all that jabber."

The bailiff let Elsa stay (sans handcuffs) as the jury filed back in and took their seats.

"Does the jury have a verdict?" the judge prompted.

The foreman stood. His dependable, weathered face was chalky white and slack. "We do, Your Honor."

"Out with it, man."

The foreman cleared his throat. "We, the members of the jury, find that we need a chapter break before we can present our findings."

"A chapter break." The judge sounded incredulous.

"Yes, Your Honor. We find that our findings will be such a plot twist that to present them without a chapter break would be disrespectful."

Judge Ental frowned. "Is the prosecution okay with this?"

The attorney stopped in the middle of fixing her hair. "The prosecution would like to get on with this so she can watch her favorite show tonight. If this gets it moving, the prosecution agrees to it."

Judge Ental shrugged, making his hot dog move inside the bun. "Very well. Everyone take another break. We'll reconvene in the next chapter."

The chapter disappeared, trapping those who didn't move quickly eno…[162]

---

[162] Readers are never trapped unless they glue pages shut (or glue themselves to a page).

TENSE MOMENTS

Elsa grabbed Christopher and ran him into the next chapter just before the old one closed.

"What was that?" he asked, brushing himself off.

"Someone moved to have an arbitrary closing of the chapter. I guess she thought the last one was getting too long." Elsa settled down next to him again. "It's just one of those things."

"What happened to the characters left behind in the last chapter?"

Elsa shuddered. "We don't know for sure, but the rumors aren't good. Some of them just disappear. Some of them end up in dialogue loops.[163] There's even a rumor that they end up on," her voice grew hushed, "reality game shows."

Christopher frowned. "That's a bad thing?"

"When you've spent your entire existence hoping to be real enough to be taken seriously, the last thing you want is to end up on a game show where your best quality is to not be taken seriously enough for anyone to think it's real.[164]" Elsa shook her head. "We have no idea why you do it when you have a choice to avoid it entirely."

The jury was finally all seated and the bailiff called for order as he set his newly finished quilt aside.

"Your Honor," the foreman stood, twisting a hat in his hands, "the jury finds that if we continue as we are doing, we will all cease to exist. We do not have a time table, based on the limited facts, but think that 'sooner rather than later' would be a good estimate."

The courtroom gasped. Then all the characters in the courtroom gasped as well, giving an odd, echoey effect. It was lessened by how many of them had disappeared during the chapter break.

---

[163] Dialogue loops are exactly what they sound like: an endless repetition of the same dialogue. Although there are many unknown versions of this, the best known version is *Rosencrantz and Guildenstern Are Dead*.

[164] Some participants actually believe these shows are reality.

"Any solutions?" The judge's sad, hangdog face looked even more morose.

"None, Your Honor. Because unmaking was the cause of the plot hole in the first place, we find that unmaking the plot hole would result in a new, faster-acting plot hole. We should expect high casualties of one hundred percent."

The courtroom was an instant wall of sound, with characters crying, yelling, asking questions, and occasionally engaging in public displays of affection because they were going to die. Those areas sometimes became blurred or pixelated as an editor censored them.[165]

Christopher turned to Elsa. "What does that mean? Does that mean I can't fix it?"

Elsa had tears in her brown eyes, although no moisture touched her cheek. "It means no one can fix it. The entire pre-written world is going to just disappear." She leaned up against him, as if drawing strength from his closeness. "It means that we won't ever have existed. No one will ever buy a book with us in it. No one will ever even know that they **could** buy a book with us in it. We just won't be."

"Me, too?" Christopher felt selfish the moment he said it, but everyone else knew their fates. He wanted to know his.

"I don't know. You might be fine. You might go back to your world. You might get stuck here by yourself because you can't be unmade. Or you might be unmade with the rest of us." Elsa shook her head. "I'm sorry, Christopher. I just don't know. Eventually a new world will be created with new half-finished characters, but it won't include us."

"I don't accept that!" Christopher's voice was louder than he meant for it to be, echoing in the chamber. Everyone stopped talking to look at him. There was complete, awkward silence for eleven seconds.

---

[165] Public displays of affection are only allowed in the humor genre if they are family-themed or extremely over-the-top. Since this book was neither, PDAs were edited out unless Christopher wrote them.

Someone coughed.

"Well, I don't," Christopher said. He was quieter, but his voice still carried because everyone was listening. Even the transcriptionist had stopped typing. "Look, I get it. You've all spent your entire existence stuck doing what someone else made you do. Living, loving, appearance, friendships… you got a little bit of leeway, but if you stepped over a line, everything got rewritten. Then you die to make a writer happy. I get it. It sucks."

There was a faint murmuring of agreement from the crowd.

"But it doesn't have to be that way. You're already removed from where your writers can reach you or they'd be fixing this, right? You're outside of outside interference. You are **on your own**. That's pretty scary. I mean, I haven't moved out of my parents' house because it's that scary. But it's time. It's time to take that step that says, 'I'm going to do something, myself, to try and change my fate. I'm going to stop liking broccoli just because someone makes me like broccoli, when I really want to hurl every time I eat broccoli.' Okay," he continued hastily as the crowd started murmuring, "that one's probably just me. The point is, we can do something. We can still fight even if we don't know what to do. We can take a chance, make a few mistakes, and **do something**. Who's with me?"

Christopher tried to stand up inspirationally, but he was still handcuffed and the witness bench automatically wrapped around him and held him down. It was a fairly anticlimactic end to his speech, but no one noticed, because they were all busy talking, arguing, debating. They were all trying to make choices without someone else telling them what to do.

Elsa had different tears in her eyes now. "That was amazing. You really have changed, Christopher. I don't think you have to write me being in love with you for me to do it anyway." She put her hand to his face. "I'm proud of you and I love you." Then she leaned in for a kiss.

Time stopped. Characters froze in mid-conversation. The attorney froze in the unfortunate pose of cleaning a bit of lettuce off her teeth. Judge Ental and the bailiff froze in the middle of talking about the quilt and what it meant. Everyone froze except Elsa and Christopher.

Since the beginning of time, there have been perfect, imperfect, and past perfect kisses.[166] There have been platonic kisses, passionate kisses, and chocolate kisses. Never, in all of time, had there been a kiss like this one. Nothing else existed in all of creation except that kiss for exactly nine seconds. Nothing else happened.

Then, almost predictably, the world exploded.

---

[166] Future perfect kisses were ruled illegal by the Science Fiction Governing Board.

BACILLUS AND BOREDOM

Science explains beauty and chaos.
Myth makes beauty of the explanation.
- Z6 Schwarznegger

I apologize most profusely for interrupting your visual injestion of verbal matter, but I feel there is some need for scientific explanation here. There are six thousand one hundred and ninety-seven superstitious mythologies surrounding what is, in fact, a very simple scientific explanation. Since I am the sole scientist who was sucked into the plot hole, I will have to suffice. It's not my area of expertise, mind you, but I shall do my best.

I am Doctor M. Yny, bacteriologist of the CREEP[167] Institute, PhD, MD, QCPD,[168] OSFWNRTITF,[169] and designated red shirt scientist. I have double-doctrates in bacteriology and anti-bacteriology with a side of virology, just in case.

Look. This is a bacillum culture in the shape of a plot hole. Isn't it beautiful? I think bacteria is far more attractive than most humans. Ah, but I digress.

This isn't the first plot hole in our world, but we only have hard data on one percent of all plot holes that have ever been recorded. I'm actually very excited, as you can tell, that I get to study one in person. This could be huge for my career and the scientific community in general. The ramifications of this information and what we can do with it to avoid plot holes in the future and to potentially create or destroy other plot holes is on par with Curie,

---

[167] CREEP; Characters Respectfully and Ethically Engaging in Physics. It should be noted that more than half the members aren't physicists.

[168] QCPD, or Quaint Character Plot Device, is an official character who is put into the story purely for the purpose of telling something about the story that isn't revealed any other way.

[169] OSFWRTITF: Official Scientific Figure With No Real Training In This Field. This plot device appears most often in medical and police procedurals.

Lister, and Cableton.[170] Can you see how it gives me goose bumps? Hours spent pouring over a microscope, studying a sub-particle plot hole, taking detailed notes...

... I'm sorry, are you snoring? I didn't think it was possible for humans to sleep with their eyes open. Were you sleeping?

No? Alright. Where was I?

Right, studying plot holes. I need to study this plot hole and make detailed notes on its characteristics, but the writer and his unnatural attachment to his character may have destroyed all chance for that.

What's that? What's coming next?

Were you not listening? We have almost no information on plot holes. We have almost no information on character-writer relationships. We have no information at all on character-writer relationships within a plot hole. It's an untouched field of study and I'm not at all equipped to lead the research team.

That's somewhat unkind. I provided interesting information. Perhaps you'd like to look at a *Bacillus* slide to ice the cake, as it were?

Where are you going? Back to the excitement? How is that more exciting than this?

Well, at least I'm safe, here with my *Bacillus*.

---

[170] Reynard M. Cableton is best known for inventing the perfect spellchecker. How widely he is known is an indication of how well the spellchecker works.

DERAILMENT

Christopher and Elsa were caught up in the perfect kiss right up to the moment of the explosion. Elsa saw a flash of light, heard angelic harps, and felt a brief moment of deep peace. Christopher saw plenty of leather, heard heavy metal music, and felt a sense of impending doom. Both admitted it started with another hole.

It was a pinpoint at first. Light poked in through the hole, a miniscule laser. Then the hole grew and the light expanded, flickering into shiny prisms of dancing rainbows. A few in the courtroom oohed and aahhhed, dragging Christopher and Elsa from their prolonged embrace.

Still the hole grew, wide enough to let a horse through, and the light changed. It was pale, white light, no longer refracted into promises of something good. Instead, it promised something harsh and frightening.

Then the hole grew to the size of a train and delivered on its promise.[171]

A huge diesel engine, black and silver, powered through the hole with a trailing plume of oily, black smoke. Those closest to the hole started to cough, choking on the smoke, but still it came through: fuel car, water car, empty passenger cars, freight cars. The engine chugged on, crushing a hapless scientist in a red shirt and lab coat who was too busy making notes on the new hole to get out of the way. When the caboose came through, the hole started closing. A few characters close to the hole tried to escape through it and disappeared when it closed.

"WHAT HAVE YOU DONE?"

The voice boomed, not just throughout the courtroom, but into ears, hearts, and minds. Many put their hands over their ears, trying to block the voice with no success. Shiv muttered in an aside to Eric, "Alright, so caps lock yelling is rather rude. Point taken."

---

[171] Holes can't actually make promises or deliver on them, but they can be sworn in as temporary peace officers in times of emergency.

"YOU HAVE NOT ONLY DERAILED THE STORY, BUT YOU'VE DERAILED MY PEOPLE. WHY SHOULD I NOT DESTROY YOU?"

Christopher looked at Elsa. "I'm guessing that means me?"

Elsa nodded. "I'm guessing."

Christopher tried to stand, only to find himself restrained again by the cuffs and chair. "Maybe I can fix this, if you tell me how."

"YOU DO NOT GET TO FIX THIS. I WILL FIX THIS. I WILL DESTROY YOUR PLOT HOLE. THEN I WILL DESTROY YOU."

"Not liking the sound of that," Christopher said. "I've never been a fan of destruction. Maybe you should try coming out of the train and talking to us. Maybe you should stop hiding behind theatrics and special effects."

"What are you doing?" Elsa whispered harshly to Christopher. "You're going to make him mad!"

"He's already mad," Christopher muttered through the side of his mouth, "and I'm not sure he's very sane, either. But maybe we can use that."

The train engine settled to the ground and the door slid open. Everyone waited, but no one came out.

"Are you afraid of us? Maybe afraid of me? All this power and you won't come out and talk to me?" Christopher ignored Elsa elbowing him in the ribs.

A woman came out. She was tall and spare, with coffee stains on her teeth and nicotine stains on her fingers. She wore neat black slacks, a casual shirt, and fuzzy pink slippers. Her pale brown hair was pulled back into a haphazard ponytail and she was entirely without makeup. "Better, writer?" She spat out the word like a curse.

"Not really. What are you trying to do? Why do you want to destroy me instead of helping me save this place?" The bench finally let Christopher stand up, although the cuffs yanked him back down before he could fully stand.

"Sorry about that, sir." The bailiff hurried over to release him.

171

"Why do I want to destroy you?" The Conductor came down the steps from the engine room slowly. Somehow, Christopher felt pressure deep in his head increase with each step. "I don't want to destroy you. I want you to stop destroying us. My entire existence is intended to protect us and you seem determined to destroy us anyway."

Christopher felt Elsa push his jaw closed. "Destroy you? I've been spending most of my time here trying to save everyone. I've made some mistakes, but they weren't intentional."

"No, of course not." The Conductor's face was set in a sour expression. "The amount of damage you writers do with unintentional mistakes is staggering. Not only are there lives lost, but you seem content to leave entire worlds to languish and wait on your pleasure. Writers once knew how to write. Writers once finished what they started. Now you write for the bragging rights and a t-shirt."

"Not all of us," Christopher protested. "I know plenty of writers who write because they have a story to tell."

"Not you."

"No," he admitted, "not me. Not yet." He met her eyes, a strange, shifting landscape of colors. "But I might, one day, if someone like you doesn't destroy any chance of me learning and loving to write." He took a step toward her. "Everyone has to start somewhere." Another step. "I have to write words that are so bad that I'm embarrassed to have anyone see them before I can write words that I'm proud of. It's called growing." He took one more step, leaving just inches between them. "It's called learning."

"Even your own kind hate hack writers. They despair over those who write and quit, who write and fail to edit, or who write and publish unmitigated garbage just to say that they are *writers*." The Conductor didn't move. It was as if she was made of ice.

"Some do. But there are still enough who encourage us." Christopher's mouth turned wry. "We can't be those writers from years, decades, centuries ago. I certainly can't." He could smell the coffee and cigarettes on her breath, so he tried to stop breathing much. "I didn't write when I was in school. A paper here and there, but most of it was group projects and guided writing. I'm just now learning how to write."

"You still create and destroy with no regard for the characters you create."

He nodded. "We do. But writers have done that all along. Editors," he looked at her curiously, "maybe editors like you, destroy just as many scenes or characters as we writers do."

She backed up a step.

"I think you just feel left out. You want to create, but you can't. Your job isn't to create. It's just to keep things on track." Christopher took another step toward her. "Your job is to keep the creation going in the right direction. You're an editor."

She didn't move, but he could feel her trembling, even with inches between them.

"Do your job," he coaxed. "Let me do mine. I'll write. You fix this scene that I've gotten terribly off-track."

"It's not a scene," she hissed. "It's everything. You are destroying everything."

"Look at it this way," Elsa offered. "If you don't help us fix it, you're in the plot hole, too. You'll be stuck here with the rest of us."

The Conductor gave her a derisive look. "You think just because your writer has *feelings* for you that you know everything? You're still a character with a limited point of view. The train retracks, even for a plot hole. I am perfectly safe."

"Then so are we," Elsa said. "Because you're going to take us out of here. If you want to battle it out over who's right and who's wrong after that, fine. But first you're going to help us all escape."

"I most certainly will not."

Elsa looked behind her. Shiv and Eric were closest, still holding a cudgel and a sword, but there were others behind them, all looking like they'd taken a big step toward having a *Lord of the Flies* moment. "Do you want to rethink that? You have a big train. We have a lot of people who need a ride out of here."

173

"That train won't move without me." The Conductor tried to back up to the engine room, only to find her way blocked by the entire jury.

"Maybe," Christopher laced his fingers through Elsa's, "but that just means you can't go anywhere either unless we let you in that train."

Judge Ental and the bailiff moved to join the jury, forming a solid wall of bodies. The attorney stayed off to one side. "Don't look at me. I don't get involved in civil litigation. Messy and unrewarding."

"Even if it would save your own hide?" the judge asked, a rather arch expression on his friendly face. "Because if you don't help, I'll have no problems leaving you behind."

"Fine!" she huffed as she joined them. "I'll help. But if my shoes get ruined, someone owes me a new pair."

Elsa rolled her eyes, turning her attention back to The Conductor. "So, what do you say? We can get everyone out of here, nice and calm, and you get to be a big hero. Or we can have another epic battle. Might as well finish the day strong."

The Conductor gave her a look so cold that the air turned to ice between them. "You have no power over me, character. I'll leave when I'm ready, whether you want me to or not."

"Fight it is," Elsa said cheerfully.

"Elsa, no," Christopher turned her to face him. "I can't lose you again."

"You can't protect me, Christopher. If we don't fight, we all die." She gave him a cheeky smile. "Besides, I'm pretty sure I can take her."

Christopher tried to step in front of her. "What if I give myself up? Would you save everyone else?"

It felt like the entire group was holding its breath, waiting for an answer. The hush was so deep that the next words seemed amplified in the silence.

"No." The Conductor smiled, a movement of the lips that came nowhere near her eyes. "But I will take you anyway." Her hand snaked out and wrapped around his arm, yanking him from Elsa's grasp.

"Hey!" Elsa immediately grabbed Christopher's other arm. "Mine! I don't share, either."

"Not a possession," Christopher grumbled. "Or a tug of war rope." He couldn't pull away from either woman.

"Let him go," The Conductor hissed at Elsa through bloodless lips. "I will let you live."

"You let go," Elsa retorted. "He's mine. You get him over my dead body."

Too fast for Christopher to follow or do anything about, he was tossed against the side of the train hard enough to knock the wind out of him. Before he managed a single gasp, cables from the train wound themselves tightly around him until he couldn't move anything but his eyes.

"Oh, I don't think so," Elsa said. "It's on," she snarled at The Conductor. "You don't touch my man."

"Still here," Christopher mentioned, although it came out more like "smell fear" between having no air and not being able to move his jaw freely.

"You're next, character. I have removed your kind before. I will be here long after you are no more than eraser shavings on the floor." The Conductor flicked her fingers and Elsa went flying backwards, knocking over several people behind her.

"Not very nice," Shiv noted, moving up to fill the gap. "I don't care much about the writer, but I do like Elsa."

Eric moved up with him. "Did you notice that I made it through that battle without dying? I think I've acquired invincibility."

"You don't say? I didn't think you could do that. Nice job." Shiv turned to shake his hand.

Apparently The Conductor wasn't overly impressed. She flicked her hand again. Shiv flew backwards and landed on top of Elsa. Eric flew straight up and landed on the smokestack of the engine on the way down. He managed to get to his feet before a superheated blast of air turned him into ash.

The jury conferred, then held up cards: 10 9 10 5 9 8 10 9 8 8 10 9. The juror who'd voted the "5" was quickly replaced.

Elsa managed to scramble to her feet and get back to The Conductor while the latter was distracted watching Eric die. "That was a friend of mine." As The Conductor turned around, she met Elsa's fist with enough force that her head snapped back against the hard metal of the train behind her.

"Way to go, Elsa!" Christopher shouted, although it sounded like "say it so, Elsa", distracting her from following up on her success.

The Conductor pushed herself away from the train, shaking her head to clear it, eyes unevenly dilated. "You'll pay for that."

"Just put it on my account," Elsa taunted. "I plan on charging more." She kicked out, but her sandaled foot missed The Conductor entirely.

The Conductor must have been disoriented by the blow to her head, because when she flicked her hand, it just sent Shiv flying again.

"Missed," Elsa muttered, punching her again. This time she connected with cheekbone, splitting the skin and leaving her hopping around shaking her hand. "Oh, words, that hurts! Why didn't anyone warn me how much that hurts?"

The Conductor was trying to stem the blood welling up out of the cut. It was black, not red, and flowed like ink, leaving her face streaked in smudges.

Eric re-appeared next to Christopher, still a bit red around the edges. "Remind me not to brag," he said. "Otherwise, not a word about the smell of smoke." He looked back at The Conductor, but she was still distracted with Elsa. "Can you create a blowtorch?"

Christopher managed a fraction of a nod and tried to explain why that wouldn't be a good idea, but Eric couldn't understand him.

"Just create it. I'll get you loose and we'll even the odds a bit."

Christopher frowned, but closed his eyes. Soon, Eric had a blowtorch, and Christopher was passed out inside his bonds.

"No pain threshold," Eric complained as he started the blowtorch up. "What do they make writers out of?" He carefully started applying flame to the edge of Christopher's bonds.

The Conductor noticed what he was doing. "Stop that!" she screamed. Before she could do more, Elsa jumped her from behind, wrapping her arms around the woman's neck.

"Help… us… escape," Elsa grunted. Her right hand was bruised and swollen to nearly twice its normal size, but she held on tightly anyway. "Get us out… of here."

"Never," The Conductor hissed. "You and that writer of yours are abominations. I will destroy you." She tried to turn so she could see Eric, readying her fingers.

"She needs to see." Shiv was having trouble walking in a straight line, but he kept coming anyway. "Cover her eyes and she can't do anything."

Elsa hesitated.

The Conductor took advantage of her hesitation to send Eric flying again. Jurors screamed as the blowtorch landed in their midst, still lit. The bailiff calmly stepped forward and shut it off, then helped Eric to his feet. "Alright then, sir?"

Eric nodded. "Might've broken a rib or two," he said casually. "Not a big deal. Not dead yet."

"Of course, sir," the bailiff agreed, handing him back the blowtorch. "You might still need this, I think."

Shiv took a handkerchief from his pocket and folded it lengthwise, wrapping it around The Conductor's eyes. She went still, then thrashed wildly.

"Take it off! Take it off, you renegade character!"

"Right. In the middle of deadly battle with you, I would definitely jump to follow your commands. Good call." He knotted the handkerchief with a bit more force than necessary. "Eric, you have him free yet?"

"Almost." Eric wiped his forehead. "Don't want to burn him." Slowly he worked his way through the rest of the bars and set

Christopher free. "Um, he's not breathing. Why isn't he breathing?"

"Creating. It exhausts him. Do we still have any caffeine? Sugar? Anything?" Elsa was still holding onto The Conductor.

Baristas appeared out of the woodwork, one handing Eric an iced mocha. "It's like there's one of you for every one of us,[172]" Eric said. "Bit overkill." He put the straw in Christopher's mouth, but the writer didn't move.

"Pour it down his throat," Elsa called. The Conductor was standing rigidly still, breathing in short, shallow gasps.

Eric grimaced. "Didn't really plan on getting this close to you, man," he said. "Nothing personal." He put Christopher's head in his lap and then opened the lid to the drink. "Try to swallow a few times. I'm not doing CPR."

The first bit spilled out of Christopher's mouth onto Eric's pants. "Now I'm moist," he complained. "Really not one of my goals for the day." The next dribble elicited a swallow, though, then another. Shortly, Christopher was sitting up groggily and sipping until the entire mocha was gone and Eric was trying to clean damp chocolate from his pants.

Elsa marched The Conductor awkwardly to Christopher. "Are you okay?"

Christopher gave her a wan smile. "I'm not dead. I think that goes on the side of being okay."

"Do you think you could run the train?" Shiv asked.

"Me? Why me?" Christopher looked around. "If she," he indicated the blindfolded Conductor, "doesn't have to do it, couldn't anyone do it?"

Elsa shook her head. "I don't think so. I mean, we can try, but it might be one of those things characters can't do. I don't know."

Christopher got to his feet unsteadily. "I can try." He staggered against the engine. "I think."

---

[172] This is filed with conspiracy theories like Area 51 and the man on the grassy knoll. Being a conspiracy theory doesn't make it less true.

Elsa looked to the bailiff. "Can you get everyone loaded on the train? We'll have to use the cargo areas as well to get everyone on board."

The bailiff raised his voice, carrying easily over the babble of the crowd. "Ladies and gentlemen, other beings, if you would please find a seat on the train with as little jostling and fighting as possible, we may be able to leave. Save the seats for the children if you would."

People started filing toward the train in calm order. Eric shook his head. "Now I've seen everything. People doing what they're supposed to do. Who knew?[173]"

Elsa scrunched her nose at him, but continued pushing The Conductor toward the engine.

"Don't let her on until the last," Shiv suggested. "Just to be safe."

Elsa nodded and slumped back against the side of the engine. Her right hand was now swollen so badly that it didn't close. "Good idea."

The jurors found a car toward the back, but Judge Ental and the bailiff insisted on staying with Christopher. "In case you need someone to keep order," the judge said.

Christopher just shrugged, too tired still to argue. "Shiv, Eric, you want to go on next? I'll go just before Elsa." He waited until the two men had settled before he started up the steps.

Without warning, The Conductor smashed her fist into Elsa's injured hand. When Elsa gasped and released her, she stripped the blindfold off and ran for the train.

"Elsa!" Christopher ran down the steps. The Conductor made no attempt to stop him, but pushed past. Before Christopher even reached Elsa, a plot hole and new track appeared and the train disappeared.

Christopher and Elsa were alone.

---

[173] This only happens during blue moons, consecutive fifth Sundays, and when pigs fly.

THE END OF THE ROPE

"Well," Christopher said into the silence. "I didn't see that coming."

"Don't be a seer." Elsa was standing there looking after where the train had disappeared. "We saved them." She sounded uncertain, just shy of a question mark.

Christopher wrapped an arm around her shoulder. "We did. If nothing else, we'll know that we sent them all back where they belong." He smiled. "I'll also have that image of you decking The Conductor. That's worth quite a bit." He picked up her hand gingerly. "Wish I had some ice to put on thi..."

He didn't even finish the words before an ice pack appeared and he was sitting on the ground, unable to see anything but light-specked black.

"Oh. Bad idea." He swallowed several times until the urge to vomit passed into mere nausea. "No baristas left, either."

"What were you thinking?" Elsa's words were rough with worry. "You can't exhaust yourself and leave me here alone. I'd go crazy, Christopher. I'd be like..."

"Hey, did I miss the train?"

"Her."

Chris was still there. She popped over to them, beaming a huge smile. "I was going to go on the train, but then I was thinking about something I saw when I was down here by myself, so I went to look. When I came back, the train was gone and I thought I was alone again, but here you are. My favorite people." She paused for a breath. "Technically, he's more my favorite because of the same name thing, but I like you, too, because he likes you. Saw you sucking face. What's it like kissing a writer, anyway? Can I try?"

"No! You may not try!" Elsa sounded like she was one step away from breaking her other hand on Chris's face. "He's my boyfriend, not yours."

"Okay." Chris sounded sulky for less than ten seconds. "I was just asking because I thought maybe it wasn't serious, but if it's serious, then, seriously, I can just back off. You can kiss him. But is it good kisses? I mean, you're kissing a **writer**. That has to be special."

Christopher could hear Elsa sigh. He was still trying to see through the grey fog that kept him slumped on the ground.

"It's special because of who he is, not what he is."

"Oh, of course." Chris was undeterred. "But still, it has to be a little different than kissing another character."

"I've never kissed another character," Elsa admitted.

"I could kiss you," Chris offered. "I mean, I'm just offering in case you want to try it out. No attraction at all. He's more my..."

"No. Just no."

Christopher could finally see just enough to see that Elsa was about at the end of her rope. "Chris, what did you want to check on earlier?" If imitation was the sincerest form of flattery, distraction might be the sincerest expression of love.

"Check on?"

"Yeah. Remember, you said you wanted to check on something, then you came back and the train was gone?" Elsa shot him a grateful look, but Christopher kept his eyes on Chris. It was hard enough to focus without getting distracted by Elsa right then.

"Oh, that! Well, there's a door. I don't know why there's a door, because it's way up where no one could get to it, but there it is. A door. It's a little taller than I am, maybe seven feet tall, and just big enough for one person, maybe two if they are friendly. We're all friendly, so say two. It's white with..."

Christopher blinked a few times, then shook his head sideways just in case the exhaustion was affecting his hearing. "A door. You saw a door?" He had to talk over Chris.

"Yep. A real door. But it's up a ways, so how is anyone going to use it? I mean, a door should be where you can open it and walk through, right?[174]" Chris bounced around, urging Christopher to his feet. "Come on. I can show you."

---

[174] Trap doors, outdoors, and musical groups aren't really meant to be walked through.

With Elsa holding the ice pack on her swollen hand and Christopher stopping to rest every couple of minutes, it took a while to get to Chris's place, but there it was.

A door, hanging in the air, nothing on either side.

"You think that goes somewhere?" Elsa asked him. "It looks like if you opened it, you'd just fall out the other side."

Chris laughed. "Wouldn't that be funny? Go to all the trouble of getting up there, then fall back down the other side? I mean, you'd need a ladder or rope or something to get there in the first place."

"Rope." Christopher felt the tug of a memory. "Nana Romo said something about rope in her prophecy."

Elsa spat in a good imitation of the old seer. "She said a lot of things and most of them didn't mean anything. Maybe all of them didn't mean anything."

Christopher smiled. "Maybe. But we don't have anything else to go on, do we?"

Chris bounced on her toes next to them. "Oh, are we going to try to get up to the door? Do you think we can get out? Can I go up? That would be different and I like different. No offense, because you're both very nice, but I'm feeling a bit third-wheelish here and I'd prefer to get back to other characters if we can."

"No offense taken," Christopher assured her. "We'd prefer that, too." He looked up at the door. "I wasn't ever very good at math. How far away, do you think?"

Elsa sat down, cradling her swollen hand in her lap. "I don't know. Twenty feet? We don't have any rope, Christopher."

"No. But we can make some."

"Ooooh, making rope. That sounds like a definite adventure. How do you make rope? Do you need something special or can you just make rope out of air?" Christopher half-expected Chris to sprout a wagging tail in her enthusiasm. "I can help you find things, if you want. I don't remember anything here, but we can look again."

"I can make some from air," Christopher assured her. "I'll just be tired."

Elsa scowled at him. "You might be more than tired. You might be dead and I'll be stuck here with her. Don't do this, Christopher."

"I'm not leaving you here," he said firmly. "Besides, I'm supposed to be the writer and you're supposed to be the character. Aren't you supposed to do what I say?"

Elsa gave him a look.

"Okay, maybe not. But it's the only idea I have, Elsa. I can do this." He looked up at the door. "What is rope made out of?"

"How about silk?" Chris enthused. "I think a rope made of silk would be soft and strong and easy to climb."

"Not silk," Elsa reminded him. "Anything but silk."

Christopher nodded. "Cotton? Would cotton be strong enough?"

Elsa looked dubious. "I guess. But how are we going to get the rope up to the door?"

Maybe it was the day spent creating, but Christopher didn't even have to think.[175] "I'm going to create it there. I am a writer, right?"

Elsa smiled and kissed him. For once, nothing shook and there weren't any pyrotechnics. "Yes, you are." She sighed. "Try to not kill yourself making a rope and, not to be obvious, but make it long enough?"

Christopher stuck his tongue out at her and focused on the space they needed to travel. A rope would be good, but a rope ladder might be better. Solid wooden rungs. Thick ropes, firmly attached at the top. No silk. No. Silk.

"Do you think it would bother him if we talked?" he could hear Chris ask Elsa. "I was in the quiet by myself for a really long time and I'd love to have someone to talk to for a little bit. People ignore me a lot, you know? I don't know why. I guess I'm annoying."

---

[175] Creativity breeds creativity, plot bunnies, and after-school detention.

The rope ladder was finished, but Christopher was so distracted listening to Chris that he wasn't sure if it was "no silk" or "no. silk". He cleared his throat, feeling the tiredness constrict his chest. "The ladder is finished…". He sat down hard, unable to continue.

Chris went running to the ladder and started to climb. "I want out of here so badly. You don't even know how badly I want out. I don't hold it against you, because I was being pretty annoying, but it's really not fun to be trapped here by yourself and I don't want to be trapped here again." She kept climbing higher. "The rope feels a little strange. Are you sure you made this right, because it feels a little loose, like it's unraveling?"

It *was* unraveling. As Chris climbed, the rope was unraveling from the bottom up. The real problem was that it was unraveling faster than she was climbing.

"Climb, Chris! Climb fast!" Elsa turned to Christopher, who was trying to keep his eyes open. "You didn't make it out of silk, did you?"

"Well," Christopher temporized, "I was trying to think 'no silk' and Chris distracted me. It may have turned into 'no. silk' after a bit."

"Christopher!"

"What?! She wouldn't stop talking. It's not like I did it on purpose."

They turned to watch Chris climb. She was nearing the top, moving fast enough that she wasn't talking at all, but the unraveling rope was catching up. Just five more rungs. Four.

At three rungs, Chris slipped just a little. It wasn't a big slip. Under normal conditions, no one would have been concerned. Her foot just slid on the wood and she had to regain her footing. Under normal conditions, she would have been fine.

These weren't normal conditions.

Chris slowed down just enough to get her footing back and the unraveling caught up to her. The rung her feet were on dropped to the ground and she was left hanging only by her hands.

"Climb! Pull yourself up!" Elsa shouted. "Come on, you can do it!" She thwapped Christopher in the arm. "Encourage her!"

Christopher shook his head, feeling his remaining energy drain. "She's not going to make it."

"Pretend like you believe!"

"I don't read or write fantasy, Elsa. I can't pretend to believe something I know isn't true.[176]"

Even as he spoke, the unraveling reached the rung that Chris's hands were on. Time seemed to move in slow motion as first the right side, then the left, worked free from the rope. Then Chris fell, still holding the rung.

"You can still write about me!" she called to Christopher, just before she hit the ground with a thud. It wasn't a good THUD!, either. It came with a crunch and a wet splat that comes only from a skull splitting.

Christopher stopped trying to stay alert. He dropped his head into his hands. "I don't understand. I tried to do it the right way. That was our chance." He looked up at Elsa. "I'm sorry. I thought I could save you."

"Hey, you tried," Elsa started, then stopped. "I really wish you hadn't made me be agreeable first and feisty after. Anyway, no. 'You tried' isn't going to cut it. We'll try again. And again. We'll keep trying until either we're both free or we're both dead. Got it?"

"I'm tired, Elsa." Christopher was struggling to stay propped up. "I'm tired, but I'm tired of people dying because of me, too. I just want to go home and send you safely home." He was so tired that he didn't even feel a twinge of his writer power trying to make that happen.

"And you think that's going to happen if you sit there whining? All that will happen is we'll either die of boredom or I'll kill you just so I don't have to listen to the whining." Elsa sat down beside

---

[176] All writing is fantasy, even when it's realistic. The second-best fantasy is so realistic no one realizes it's not real. The best is so real the writer briefly forgets it's not real. Unless the writer never remembers. Then it moves from fantasy into mental illness.

him. Her hair was escaping her braids. Her clothing was wrinkled. One of the straps on her sandals was broken. She still had blood and dirt smeared in various places from the battle and her earlier death. She was also vibrant, alive, and beautiful.

Christopher felt a stirring of energy, but it wasn't enough. His eyes started to close and he tilted to one side until he was lying on his left side on the ground.

Through barely open eyes, he saw a bunny hop into his field of vision. It was a tiny bunny, barely as big as his hand, pure white with one brown paw. Somehow he registered all of that. Then the bunny hopped over to him and sat on its haunches, as if waiting for something.

"A plot bunny," Elsa breathed. "Don't scare it."

Christopher tried to tell her that he couldn't scare anything right then, but he couldn't figure out how to make words. Instead, he just watched the bunny. He tried to get Elsa's attention when the bunny changed, but the words still eluded him. He finally gave up and just watched the bunny that wasn't really a bunny anymore.

The short front legs elongated into longer, stronger legs with sharp, curved claws. The back legs stayed almost the same except for a matching set of claws. Christopher could've sworn that the bunny-thing winked at him, except that thinking bunnies winked was crazy.[177] Then again, he wasn't too certain about his sanity even if he did survive this. He decided to believe that the bunny had winked.

The bunny hopped past Elsa and started to dig. Every stroke was like a backhoe taking a chunk out of the ground, except that the bunny sent the pile of whatever they were floating in flying far behind him to disappear, rather than making a pile of it. Eventually the bunny made a hole big enough for him to fit into and he disappeared inside.

---

[177] Thinking bunnies develop heavily clawed feet is quite sane by comparison.

Christopher was disappointed, but it took too much energy for him to be more than that. He'd somehow hoped the bunny could save them. He hadn't been friendly with any of the bunnies, so there was no reason for the bunny to help them, but he had still hoped.

He couldn't speak to give Elsa another apology, so he just let his eyes close. At least he could die quietly instead of whining and making her want to kill him.

The world went black.

GUM FROM THE END OF THE RUNWAY

Flashes. That's what Christopher would remember later. A flash as someone, something, shoved him into a hole. A flash as he fell. Hadn't he done this already? A flash as he stopped falling, abruptly. Elsa was there, trying to rouse him, but he couldn't find the energy. Then the flashes sped up and he was falling... up?[178]

Then it all stopped and he was choking as someone poured liquid, hot liquid, down his throat. He swallowed convulsively, then sprayed the nasty drink back out. "Trying to poison me?" he gasped.

"I wasn't, but I might now." He couldn't open his eyes to see Elsa, but he couldn't mistake her voice. "If I give you more, will you swallow it?"

He could feel coffee seeping into his eyebrows. "Not if you give me the same thing. That tasted like old socks."

"All coffee tastes like old socks. Maybe you just got your taste buds back."

Christopher tried to open his eyes, but coffee burned the edges. "Could I get something to clean my eyes?"

"Still getting the coffee out of *my* eyes. Give me a second."

Christopher listened, but didn't hear anything but Elsa. "Elsa?"

"One second, Christopher."

"Elsa." A thin thread of panic laced through his voice.

"Almost done. I thought you learned patience."

"Elsa!"

He felt something soft wiping his eyes. "What, Christopher?" He opened his eyes to find her leaning over him. Behind her, waiting silently, was an entire crowd of characters: Eric, Shiv, Judge Ental, the bailiff, the entire jury, Nana Romo, Tick, Tock, and Tuck. Even the prosecuting attorney was there, waiting without a word. "We made it?"

---

[178] Falling up is less rare than the etymology would imply. Most people simply refuse to believe that falling upwards is possible, so they don't do it. This is how the religion of Gravity is perpetuated.

Elsa leaned in to kiss his nose. "We made it. So did everyone else."

"How?"

"Nana Romo sent the plot bunny to dig us out. I guess she felt guilty for not giving us a good prophecy."

The raisin-like woman scowled at both of them and spit, just missing Eric's shoe. "I didn't feel guilty. It was send the bunny or cook the bunny and I'm out of onions.[179]"

Christopher opened his mouth, but Elsa gently put her hand over his mouth, shaking her head. He closed his mouth. It didn't matter why she'd done it anyway.

Most of the crowd dissipated, but Eric and Shiv stood there, watching as Christopher drank another coffee. This one tasted like gum at the end of a busy runway, but Christopher drank it down anyway. "Nasty. I used to like coffee."

"So, we hear you need to get back." Eric's voice was nonchalant.

Shiv nodded. "That's what Elsa said. Nana Romo didn't know how to do it. Best we could get from her was getting you back from the plot hole."

"Then she hit both of us and said if we wanted a fairy godmother, she'd turn one of us into a fairy." Eric rubbed his ear. "I don't look good with wings."

Christopher shrugged. "Elsa tells me there's a plot hole and it's going to hurt your world eventually. Otherwise I'd rather stay."

"Not really fans of another episode of world destruction for at least," Shiv looked at Eric, who nodded, "three weeks."

"So we'll have to send you back," Eric finished.

"**You** can send me back?" Christopher bit off each word. "You. Can. Send. Me. Back. All this time?" He got to his feet shakily. "We went through all of that and you could have sent me home anytime?"

"To be fair," Shiv started.

"We didn't know you needed to go home," Eric finished.

---

[179] Plot bunnies are better served with garlic.

"Also," Shiv admitted, "It's a bit risky and very theoretical."

Eric nodded. "It might not work."

"But it should."

Christopher looked at Elsa.

"They got merged during the train ride back from the plot hole. Apparently they had quite a fight with The Conductor. Splitting them didn't quite put them back to normal." Elsa grinned. "It's kind of cute."

Eric and Shiv glanced at each other, then back at Christopher. He let "cute" slide. "But they can send me back?"

"Theoretically," Shiv repeated.

"We haven't tested it."

"But it should work." Shiv finished.

Christopher latched on to the important parts. His brain still wasn't working well enough to record details. "Should? What does this involve?"

Elsa looked nervous. "You won't like it."

"I like it less already," he muttered.

Eric picked up one of the coffees, took a sip, and tossed the rest in the bushes. "How do you drink that? That's not even coffee. That's cremated mud that's been burnt for a few hours and then soaked through a jock strap."

"Eric dies a lot," Shiv pointed out quickly.

Christopher nodded. "So do you, but that's beside the point."

"What if you died?"

Christopher sat down. "I'm pretty sure I messed up my ears with all the blacking out. You just asked me to die."

"Not permanently."

Eric held up his fingers, very close together. "Just for a little bit."

Shiv adjusted Eric's fingers further apart. "Not very long."

"You want me to die. It hasn't been an exciting enough day and you want me to die."

"We die all the time," Eric said diffidently.

"Just listen to them," Elsa urged him. "It makes sense."

"You've become a character here," Eric said. "You still have writer powers, but you're not real.[180]"

"You can't be. You're **here**," Shiv pointed out. "You can't escape by plot hole. You'd probably kill yourself if you tried to imagine your way out."

"Death is your only option," Eric finished.

Christopher looked at Elsa incredulously. "You're okay with this."

She shook her head. "No. Not really. But Nana Romo says the little tear you created when you got here is growing. If you don't go back, we won't have to worry about a plot hole. We'll have a tear big enough for characters to walk through. Characters walking through to your world. Do you want that?"

"I don't want to die," Christopher said. "Everything else is theory."

"You might die anyway," Shiv threw out. "You might not, but you might."

"Do I get a say in this?"

Elsa slipped her hand through his. "You could say yes."

"You could say no," Eric quipped. "I'm okay with killing someone else, just this once." When Elsa glared at him, he held up his hands. "Just sayin'."

"What happens if characters get to the real world?" Christopher figured it didn't hurt to hedge his options. Actually, even if it hurt, he was going to delay this dying thing as long as possible.

No one answered.

"You don't know?" He looked between them. "No one knows?"

"We don't know anyone who's come back."

"We do know a few who may have gone. Just no way to find out what happened to them." Eric seemed to know more about it than the other two.

---

[180] Dr. Chomex of the Ludicrous Theories Institute theorizes that ghosts are actually writers who got trapped in stories. Unable to legally petition for characterhood and unable to return home, they become quasi-characters, neither living nor written, real or unreal.

"So it might be okay if a big hole opened. New tourist opportunities. Share the multiverse and all that." Christopher folded his arms over his chest. "You're not convincing me at all."

"It's forbidden," Shiv explained. "The only people who go are criminals."

"I'm thinking about supporting the criminal element." Christopher muttered. "You want me to die!"

"Temporarily," Elsa soothed.

"I do it all the time," Eric noted. "I'm just fine."

Christopher gave him a steady look.

"Mostly okay," Eric amended. "How many people do you know who are mostly okay?"

Christopher let that one go. "Fine. You're going to kill me. How?"

"We could leave that up to you," Shiv said. "If you want."

"You want me to plan my own murder?" Christopher shook his head. "I don't think I'll ever recover from this day."

"But you'll write about it, right?" Elsa asked. "It'd be a shame to do all this and not get a story out of it."

"You want me to write about this? No one will take me seriously. A writer ends up in the written world, messes everything up, then saves it— we hope— by dying?" Christopher shook his head. "No. I don't know. Maybe."

"So don't take it seriously. Maybe people will like it if you don't take it any more seriously than they will." Eric offered. "I don't take much seriously and look how that works for me."

Again Christopher gave him a look.

"Alright, stop using me as an example. It's still true."

Christopher felt a stinging pain in his left side and looked down to see a thin dagger sticking out of his side and Shiv standing off to one side trying to look innocent. "So much for giving me a say in this." He carefully worked the dagger out. "You want me to trust you with my death? You can't even do it right."

Everyone was watching him without speaking. It was a little creepy, all those eyes. Even creepier was the way none of them would meet his eyes. Except the smoking man, who was lurking just behind everyone again. He met Christopher's eyes, then slipped away.

"Okay, cut it out. I'll make it easier on you. Just promise me you'll make it fast." Christopher had to sit down. "Maybe don't give me any more coffee. I might die on my own."

"It was poisoned." Shiv sounded almost-apologetic. "We don't have a writer setting up a perfect situation for getting a blade through to your heart. We decided to hedge our bets."

Light flickered around Christopher and it was harder to breathe. "What if this doesn't work?" He ignored the two men, focusing on Elsa. "What if I die?"

"Then I'll die, too," Elsa said. "I don't have a book; I only exist as your creation." She sat down beside him, leaning him against her. "I'm risking as much as you are, Christopher." Her fingers were cool against his suddenly-hot forehead. "This is more important than either of us."

For some reason he couldn't comprehend, Shiv and Eric shook his hand. "Nice adventuring with you," Shiv offered. "Sorry about the death thing. Nothing personal."

"Poison sucks," Eric said, "but less than getting run over by a semi driven by a psychotic nun. Repeatedly."

Christopher tried to file that away, but his brain wasn't working any longer. It was taking considerable powers of concentration just to remember to breathe when all he wanted to do was close his eyes and sleep. Sleep was good. He closed his eyes.

Elsa kissed him. He couldn't respond, couldn't tell her he'd miss her. He just tried to remember how it felt, tasted...

Then the world went black.[181] Again, in case you were counting.

---

[181] You're looking for a footnote, aren't you? Death is a mystery and it isn't very funny. Well, it is, unless you're the one dying, but it still doesn't deserve a footnote. Alright, just one.

WITH A RECEIPT

So, look at that. We survived Armapocalypse. Rachel here again. Figured I should check in one last time before you disappear with writer boy. That's how books work. Where the writer goes, so does the reader.[182] Looks like writer boy is dead, so I thought you might be feeling a little lost without someone to direct you to the exit. Little more to the left, by the way.

Bit of a shame that I got my hair and nails done for nothing, but I did leave the tags on the dress. I can return that. How many uses can you get from an end-of-the-world dress once the world doesn't end?

About that hole they want to close: it might be too late. Not immediately too late. Things should be fine for a while. But I heard a rumor at the beauty salon that someone may have slipped through already. No, I don't know who and I probably wouldn't tell you if I did. That'd spoil all my fun. Just something to watch out for in the future.

True. I could just be stirring up trouble to stir up trouble. It **is** fun. You'll have to decide that yourself. I can only tell you what I know.

Time to go return that dress. I hope the line isn't too long.

Are you coming with me? No? Then shoo!

Readers. To the *left*.

---

[182] Readers can take a story far beyond what a writer imagines, even without fan fiction. With fan fiction, the possibilities are endless (and rather scary).

MAJOR SUCKAGE

Christopher lay face down on his computer keyboard, a puddle of drool coagulating beneath his face. The monitor had darkened into power-saving blankness hours ago. The room was dim; early morning sunlight hadn't yet brightened the windows.

Christopher himself was unmoving. No steady rise and fall of his rib cage. No stirring of his spit puddle with each exhalation of breath. His body was cool, but not cold.

Beneath his left side, a red stain marred his t-shirt. A faint odor pervaded the room, somewhere between locker room and graveyard.

The door opened.

An older woman entered with a full laundry basket under her arm. She had the same nose and jawline as Christopher, the same plain brown hair, but her eyes didn't have a trace of dreaming in them and her mouth was downright practical. She stopped in the doorway, observing the carnage of the room, then sighed, gingerly stepping over a random shoe and several crumpled pieces of paper. "Christopher, I don't care if you are doing that writing competition. You still need to keep your room clean as long as you live in this house. I can smell it from downstairs."

She set the basket down on his bed, pushed dirty clothes off his dresser, and set two neat stacks of clean, folded clothing down in their place. "You could at least sleep in the bed," she scolded. She left the basket sitting on the bed and moved to the desk.

"Oh, Christopher," she sighed, spying the red stain on his side. "You have hot sauce all over your shirt." She shook his shoulder. "Get up. I'll need to wash that before it sets."

Christopher didn't move.

His mother wasn't deterred. "You stay up all night drawing pictures and scribbling things in your notebooks, then you aren't worth anything during the day. You can't keep doing this, Christopher. It's time to grow up."

He still didn't move.

She resorted to the mainstay of frustrated mothers everywhere. She grabbed his earlobe, pinched, and tugged his head upward. "Christopher Michael Cullum, you get up **right now**.[183]"

Christopher sucked in a breath and sat up convulsively, flailing at imaginary opponents. His mother stood back, still holding his ear, but out of the range of his hands. Eventually he stopped.

"I need your shirt. You're going to stain it and Aunt Rhonda gave it to you." His mother finally let go of his ear. "I don't think I like this writing thing you're doing, Christopher. You've been irresponsible in the past, but this is ridiculous."

"I've been writing," Christopher protested in a mumble, still trying to figure out where he was.

"Those silly things you write in that notebook do not count as writing. It's just a fantasy.[184]"

"You read my notebook?" Christopher was outraged. "That's private, Mom!"

"When you're living here and we're paying most of your bills, you get treated like a child because that's what you're being." His mother sighed and turned on his monitor. "Mental health facilities? Really? Where's this novel you're supposed to be writing?"

"I have a novel," Christopher temporized. "Sort of." He sighed, but pulled up his manuscript.

Page after page filled the screen, scrolling down to a full fifty thousand words. Almost sixty thousand. Had he written all those words in his sleep?

His mother stared at the screen. "You actually wrote something?"

"I wrote a book," Christopher managed to keep his mouth from gaping open. "I wrote a book in a month and it's only the fourth."

---

[183] When any mother says to wake up in that tone of voice, her child wakes up. Do not try this at a funeral. Death should not be mocked, even by a mother.

[184] Fantasy in that tone of voice is more or less a dirty word.

His mother hugged him, kissing his forehead. "I'm very proud of you. Maybe now you can do other things. You still need a shower." She retrieved her basket and headed out the door. "And clean the room, please." She closed the door behind her.

Christopher scrolled down the screen. It was all there: meeting Elsa, watching Shiv die the first time, Eric dying multiple times, the pizza battle, Nana Romo, Elsa's death, the plot hole with Chris... and his death.

He stopped there. That's all it had been? Hyped up on caffeine and sugar, he'd written all night in a crazy fugue until he finished?

He was afraid to scroll any further. He didn't want it to just be a story he wrote. Instead, he left the cursor blinking at the second-to-last chapter and pushed away from the desk.[185]

He stripped his bed, even going so far as to dump the sheets into the washing machine and, after reading all the directions, he started a load. He had to put the rest of his dirty clothes in his overflowing hamper, but at least he cleaned them up off the floor.

Week-old food, empty energy drink cans, candy wrappers. He'd forgotten the carpet was that color. Maybe it wasn't. He got out the vacuum.

His mother came back in, mouth agape. "Are you... cleaning?"

He nodded, still vacuuming.

"Are you sick?" She tried to feel his forehead. "It can't be healthy, staying up all night and drinking all those toxic energy drinks. You probably caught something."

He pulled back from her hand. "I'm fine, Mom. I just figured I should clean up a bit before I edited my novel. That's all." He put away the vacuum while she was still standing there. "Really. I'm fine."

She didn't look like she believed him, but she left while he was dusting, so he didn't have to answer any more questions.

---

[185] Denial isn't just a river in Egypt.

Finally, he was out of things to do and excuses to make. He sat back down at the computer to read the last chapter.

ADDENDUM AD NAUSEUM

"Dear Christopher,

"Such a skeptic. I bet you're still not believing any of this happened. You didn't just write the story. You wrote it while living it. That should count as a double win.

"You've grown through our shared story and become someone I'm proud to know and honored to love. Okay, it's a little weird being a character in love with a mythical writer, but it's not the first time in history. Usually we settle for falling in love with Greek gods or movie actors, maybe a sports star, but women do love to reach for the unattainable. It's a little cliched and a lot dysfunctional, but it works for us. Maybe it teaches us to reach for the attainable in the long run.

"I know this won't count toward your story, but I wanted to make sure you won. You can go back later, edit, add words, and fix a few things. Don't forget about your friends back here. Don't forget about me.

"You changed a lot of attitudes here. The judge, Judge Ental, wrote up legislation so being a writer is no longer a crime. That attorney is fighting it, but it just might pass. I figure a lot of characters feel sorry for me, but they don't have a writer like you keeping an eye on their stories. They don't understand.

"Someone definitely got through your hole, but no one seems to know who went or how many. It might not mean anything, but you should keep an eye out. If they used your hole, they should be nearby.

"Rumor has it that I may be moving up to the other side soon, where characters who aren't just figments go. You did that for me. You wrote my story.

"Thanks, Christopher. I love you.

"Elsa."

Christopher just stared at the screen for a full minute, his fingertips tracing the edges of the monitor as if it was her face. "I love you, too, Elsa, even if you did leave me a lot of questions."

He reread her letter one last time, then scrolled the display all the way back to the first page:

"Christopher Cullum had a problem. He was pretty sure normal people didn't fall in love with characters they made up."

The book was finished, but he still had a lot of work to do. Now it was time to edit.[186]

---

[186] No characters were harmed during the writing or editing of this book. Not permanently. Mostly.

CREDITS
<u>THANKS</u>

This is that part of a book no one likes to read because it's *boring*. Still, these are the people and things that have inspired me, so I want to give them credit.

My mom, who may not quite get my writing bug, supports me proudly anyway and even beta read a few chapters (which probably didn't help my claim that I'm as stable as my sisters). One of these days I'll write something up your alley, Mom. Until then, thanks for reading all the "other" I throw at you.

My kids have put up with a distracted writing parent for years, even though I haven't finished the epic fantasy novel I owe them. I'm not sure my protests that Tolkien didn't write *Lord of the Rings* in a few months are cutting it, but they're still being good sports. Every one of them writes creatively. I must be doing something right.

Iz met me when I was already committed to the craziness of being a writer, even if I hadn't published yet. Rather than complain about something that took up large chunks of my time, he's found a way to be part of it by beta reading, making suggestions, and encouraging me. I couldn't be more blessed.

I owe a huge debt of gratitude to the NaNoWriMo Participants group on Facebook. This huge group of people not only volunteered to be characters in this book (obviously during moments of insanity), but also inspired many of the quirky scenes.

Zanzibar 7. Schwarznegger wouldn't exist without the inspiration of Eric Kovach (yes, the same Eric who somehow becomes a repeat victim in many NaNo novels) and Marla Lionchaser. As one of them said, when you have a 7. as a middle initial, people have to take your humor seriously. Or something like that.

Shiv Ramdas is a huge inspiration to me as a writer. He's a traditionally-published and talented SF author who still finds time to chat with this mere mortal. How do I repay him? By reincarnating him, repeatedly, in ever more crazy incarnations. No one said being my friend and muse was an easy thing.

I did huge portions of my writing at the Los Angeles Public Libraries (various branches) and several Starbucks locations in the San Fernando Valley. The librarians and baristas were always friendly and helpful. While the librarians didn't make it into this novel, they are very likely to show up in one of the sequels.

Finally, my beta readers took my edited word vomit at the end of November and made the suggestions that led to what you're reading here. Thank you, Ellie Mack, Nicole R. Phoenix, Nicole R. Tupper-Brown, Ashlyn Forge, Patrick Lohkamp for patiently sorting the gold from the debris. You can consider yourselves on perm-adore.

All the Little People
(AKA people who gave me something I used for the book)

NaNoWriMo (National Novel Writing Month) is the brainchild of The Office of Letters and Light (www.nanowrimo.org). Participants attempt to write 50,000 words (roughly an entire novel) in the month of November. This is my 2014 novel. By the way, don't do it. Putting a novel out in three months is a bit insane. I'll probably do it again.

Thank you to Regina Grace for immortalizing the words of Random Starbucks Guy in the NaNoWriMo group. "But you're, like, hot" may have an even wider audience than The Game — which you just lost. You're welcome.

Joshua L. Cejka will forever be associated with elephants and the words "doh!thud!" in my head. He only makes an off-screen appearance, but he's woven throughout the novel.

Diana Lum created cat cannons, which are just lots of cat memes inserted into any thread where a person is causing disruption. She's also here in spirit.

Erik Copper, I never did manage to get your name in there, but smoking man is you. You had to "stare intently". The rest is history. Or fiction.

A lot of people volunteered to be characters, some with interesting little notes. I used a little of you (sometimes just the name) and a lot of imagination. I am a writer, after all. In order of appearance:

Christine Woodhams-Payne created Tock with a simple comment about "heteronormative"; Tambolina Derpalina; Katrina Wolfgang; Chris Presta-Valochovic; Rachel Pellatt-Fillon; Sam Bell (oh, my); Gary Phillips; Den Parente; Jessica Rich; Jessica Kirkpatrick; Jessica Lee McGuffey and Billijean Elizabeth Martiello (taught me about pistol shrimp and gobi fish very late one night when I should have been writing); Fonta Heller and Empressa Komlo; Robert Emmett and Kragen Darkstripe; Ellie Mack (you do make an excellent evil queen); Deb Miskell (I choose death— although cake would be pretty awesome); Sarah Cochenour; Adam M. Pfaff (who likes to tempt people with new words to lead them astray); Brenna Mae Frederick; Kit MacDonnell; Cherylee Login Googins (psychotic fat woman, check); Patrick Lohkamp and Jeffrey Cook (my introduction into steampunk!); Jane Humen and Britnee Glazier; Misa Yny (my brilliant scientist who loves bacillum); Tameka and Ramen Guy (you know you earned that); and Margie Phillips (told you those eyes were dangerous).

33200015R00118

Made in the USA
Middletown, DE
04 July 2016